CHAMPION OF MIDNIGHT

Chronicles of Midnight - book 2
Debbie Cassidy

Cover by JMN Art

The drive to the House of Vitae was mostly a silent one, not for want of trying on my part, mind you, but Drayton was determined to keep conversation limited. If I'd known helping him push back his demon would result in this distance, I would have … still done it, damn it. The atmosphere was strained. The memory of what had happened in the dungeons hung between us. I'd seen him stripped bare, out of control. I'd seen the darkest part of him, and although he was grateful for my help—he'd said as much—there was obviously a part of him that was ashamed. Maybe it was time to open up and talk about it? Just push the issue and clear the air instead of tiptoeing around the subject. I slid a quick glance his way. His jaw was tense, and his eyes were on the road in total focus; a little too much focus, if you asked me. Yeah, maybe talking about stuff could wait.

It was strange having my shields partially down, but Drayton had made it clear that going to visit the Sanguinata reeking of human was a bad idea. Besides, it was best to keep the number of people who knew about my shielding ability to the minimum. Ambrosius's words echoed in my ears, his assertion that I controlled the hunger whether the shields were up or down. He'd been silent since the Arachne's attack underground. Was it strange that I missed his voice in my head?

A huge set of iron gates came into view with the words *Domus Vitae* emblazoned across a crest on their arch. The crest was a shield depicting a serpent and a sword. Neat script reading *perpetua vita aeterna et sapientia* ran along a plaque under the crest.

"Life everlasting and wisdom eternal." How the heck did I know that?

Drayton shot me a curious glance. "You learned Latin?"

I shook my head. "No. I didn't."

"Then how—"

The gates swung soundlessly inward with the help of two silent, stoic-faced guards. They stood back, stiff and distant in their purple livery, as we drove through the gates.

"We're expected," Drake explained. "I called ahead."

"You have the warrant, right?"

He nodded tightly. "I do, but they don't

know that. This is a social call." He slid a warning glance my way.

Bane had made it clear that we were to do this one by the book. "Drayton, Bane said —"

"Look, let me just try it my way first, okay?"

I blew out a breath. It was impossible to make a valid argument with so little information on the Sanguinata or this dude, Dorian. There was no choice but to follow Drayton's lead. I was a newbie to the Protectorate, and although Bane had released me for patrol, this was still meant as an observational learning exercise.

Drayton steered the Rover through the entrance and down a neat cement pathway bordered by clean, crisply kept gardens. The roses looked black and gray in the moonlight, but they grew here in abundance. The fact that any plant life grew in Midnight was still a mind boggle, but the magic of Arcadia was strongest in this district, whether due to the concentration of nephs or the ministrations of the Order of Merlin, who knew. It just was.

The driveway seemed to stretch forever. And were we on an incline? "How much farther is the house?"

Drayton's lips lifted in a wry smile. "The *house* is just over this rise."

What was with the emphasis on the word *house*? We reached the top of the rise, and my question was answered. House of Vitae was no *house*; it was a freaking castle—a castle with a huge-arse moat around it.

"Shitting hell!"

"Right?" Drayton snorted. "The Sanguinata have some serious money and clout in the city. We do *not* want to piss them off."

Good to know.

We hit the bottom of the rise, and Drayton sped up a bit down the long stretch of road leading up to the bridge spanning the moat. Water gleamed in the silvery rays of the moon. A dark shape cut through it, slipped under the bridge, and came out on the other side.

I craned my neck to try and get a better look at it, but it dove underwater. "What the heck was that?"

"Dorian's little pet."

"I would not call that *little*."

"Yeah, Mitch has grown a little since I was last here."

"Mitch?"

"That's what Dorian calls it."

"What is it?"

"I'm not entirely sure."

Great.

We slid under the archway into a stone courtyard, and Drayton parked the car. Balustrades depicting beautiful women and men in poses of a sexual nature dotted the pretty quad, and ivy crawled up the stone walls as if desperate to reach for the moon. A stone archway and a brick wall cut off the courtyard from the main castle.

We exited the vehicle and waited. Long minutes passed, and then the echo of boots filled the courtyard.

"That'll be Dorian's butler, Jeffery," Drayton said.

How many times had Drayton visited the Sanguinata, and why? A slender, somber man appeared under the arch. He stopped and pressed his heels together. "Please, do follow me."

He led us through the arch and a set of thick, wooden double doors into a brightly lit stone entranceway. Unlike the mansion, the castle was spotless and modern inside. Someone had gone to a whole lot of trouble to get this place in order. The walls had been plastered and hung with pretty landscapes and portraits of severe, beautiful people. The floors were carpeted in thick pile, muffling our footsteps as we slipped through corridors and up stairs. So many little details to take in, but my attention was on the exits—the windows that were too high up, and the doors that seemed to be locked. As we took twists and turns, my mind made a mental map in case we should need to make a hasty escape. Drayton seemed familiar with the castle, relaxed even, but I knew enough about Drayton to know how easily he could slip in and out of the chilled persona he liked to don. And with my shields semi-down, the tension buzzing beneath his mask was static against my skin.

We stepped onto a foyer on the third floor. Double doors again, this time cream with ornate brass handles, barred the way. Jeffery walked briskly toward them and flung them open.

The hum of voices and the tinkle of music drifted out to greet us, followed closely by the scent of roasted meat and something else, something coppery and tangy.

Blood.

"Master, your guests have arrived." The butler bowed and then ushered us into the room. The chamber was long, and we entered at one end. On either side were two long banquet tables occupied by nephs—Sanguinata, no doubt. Gold, cream, and crimson were the themes here, and no windows, it seemed, unless they were hidden behind the thick velvet drapes that spanned the length of the wall to our right. Heavily made-up humans dressed in flimsy garments worked the tables, serving and ... Wait, was that a Sanguinata filling her wine glass from that human's wrist?

"Stop staring," Drayton whisper-hissed.

Tearing my gaze from the display, I focused on the cream tiled walkway that cut between the tables. It led to a man lounging on what looked like a mini throne. It was even set on a dais. He was blond and powerfully built, which he obviously liked to show off, as he wasn't wearing a shirt. His eight-pack was on display, and his bare feet were propped up on a cushy footstool. A small table sporting a bowl of fruit was placed within reach. A pale, ornately-dressed woman sat on a chair to his right, and a human female sat on the floor by his throne. She was dressed almost indecently in a see-through nightgown. Her feet were also bare, and gooseflesh peppered her skin. Her hair was clean and shiny, though — the only part of her that looked healthy. Other than that, she looked like she was about to topple onto her face. Wait, what was that red pipe peeking out from under her hair?

"Drayton, how good to see you," Dorian said. "It has been too long."

"Indeed." Drayton inclined his head. "How have you been?"

"Oh, you know, surviving." He lifted something to his lips, the red pipe ... Not a pipe, a fucking straw.

He sucked on it and waved us forward. Taking my cue from Drayton, I walked closer to the imposing Sanguinata, coming to a halt about three meters away.

The human at Dorian's feet groaned, part in protest, part in ecstasy. Dorian ran a hand over her head. Her eyes rolled upward, and then her lids drooped. She slumped against his thighs. His lips turned down in disgust, and he jostled his leg, sending her toppling to the floor.

My chest tightened and I took a step forward. Drayton gripped my arm and squeezed in warning.

"I despair," Dorian drawled. "If we don't win the games this year, I fear we shall all starve."

The gathered Sanguinata chuckled, but the sound was more polite than genuine. As if laughter was the expected reaction. I thought they needed the blood to survive due to a deficiency, not to use as a food source. I tried to catch Drayton's eye, but he was resolutely fixated on Dorian.

Dorian smiled, but the action was cold and devoid of any real emotion. "Jeffery, please take this one away and bring me a fresh one."

He said it like he was asking for a refill on a cocktail. The butler reappeared as if by magic, which, who knew, it may just have been. He gathered the human into his arms without effort. She probably didn't weigh more than a child. Blood trailed from the tube, spattering the floor as he carried her from the room.

My stomach turned.

What the fuck?

The rest of the Sanguinata continued with their meals, sipping crimson fluid from crystal cut glass. Blood ... They were drinking blood, probably taken from the humans serving them. Why had I thought that humans donated blood and that was that? I'd never expected them to be treated like blood bags, to be fed off directly.

"Don't worry, little neph," Dorian said. "We do not bite."

I blinked at him. He was talking to me. "You don't?"

He shrugged. "Of course not. That would be against the district laws."

Someone to my left snickered.

Dorian was lying.

Beside me, Drayton tensed. Why wasn't he saying anything?

"So, what is the real reason for your visit, Drayton?" Dorian leaned forward, plucked a grape off the table, and popped it into his mouth. He chewed slowly. "Tell me, what is it I can help you with?"

God, I wanted to smash the smarmy look off his beautiful face.

Drayton sighed and held up his hands. "You got me, Dorian. Can't get anything past you. But it's actually something I was hoping to help *you* with. Give you a heads-up."

"Oh, really?" Dorian sat up a little straighter. "Information, eh? We love information, don't we?" He transferred his attention to his court, and a hearty murmur of agreement skittered across the gathered. "Go on."

Drayton winced. "It seems like one of your Sanguinata has been attempting to recruit humans."

Something dark flitted across Dorian's face, but it was gone too quickly, replaced by an appropriate expression of concern. "No." He placed a hand on his heart. "That cannot be true. One of mine would never break the law in such a blatant way, especially when we know what's at stake if we do."

He was lying. Again. It dripped from his voice and settled around him like a bad smell. With my shields partially down, it was easy to pick up on the untruth. Drayton tensed. Had he sensed it too?

"Well, it's happening," Drayton said. His tone remained easy and light. "We spotted him at The Deep just over a week ago."

"A week?" Dorian's brows shot up. "And you leave it till now to come and see me."

"We had another case to deal with that couldn't wait."

"Ah, yes. The underground tunnels and the monstrous spiders."

Man, news got around quick in Midnight.

"So, tell me. What did this lawbreaking Sanguinata look like? You know most of my men. Is it someone here?" He waved an arm to encompass the room. "Point him out and I shall read his memories.

They could do that?

Drayton turned to me. "Serenity?"

"You didn't personally see the lawbreaker?" Dorian said. He focused his attention on me. "Your colleague did. The *new* member of your team." He smiled, flashing fang. But while Bane's fangs gave me delicious shivers, his just turned my stomach.

"Yeah, I saw him." I lifted my chin. "I can identify him too."

I swept my gaze over the Sanguinata to my left and to my right, searching each face for the one that was etched in my mind. My brain was funny that way, capturing details like a photograph when I needed it to and, sometimes, even when I didn't.

Damn it, the culprit wasn't present. "He's not here."

Dorian stuck out his bottom lip in mock sorrow. "In the absence of a positive identification, I'm afraid all I can do is reinforce the rules at our next meet. Give the house a talking to."

"And when is the next meet?" Drayton asked evenly.

Dorian's lips twitched in amusement. He ducked his head and studied his nails. "The night before the games."

This was all a joke to him. My face heated in indignation. The fucker had no intention of doing anything to stop the illegal recruitment. Drayton had been right about being able to get him to talk without use of a warrant, but not using the warrant had also given him a sense of security. He was toying with us, thinking there was nothing more we could do. Drayton had asked me to take a back seat on this one, but there was no way I was letting that smarmy fucker get away with breaking the law. Dorian deserved a rude awakening.

I ripped the warrant from Drayton's back pocket and fanned myself with it. "Sorry, not good enough. I suggest you call a meet immediately. Now. Right here, so I can find the perpetrator and *you* can punish him."

Dorian's eyes narrowed and his lip curled. "What is the meaning of this?"

I unfolded the paper. "Oh, this?" I widened my eyes as if surprised to see the warrant in my hand. "This is a warrant giving us authority to question everyone we see and search the premises in an attempt to locate the lawbreaker."

"Serenity…" Drayton's tone was laced with warning.

"No, Drayton. We tried it your way, but this *isn't* a social call. This is official business." I crossed my arms. "I suggest you cooperate, Dorian. You wouldn't want a copy of this warrant to find its way to the House of Mort, would you?" I tapped my chin. "Wouldn't that mean forfeiting the games this year?"

Dorian's already pale expression paled even further, and the gathered broke out into excited whispers.

Dorian slumped back in his seat and waved a hand in my direction. "There is no need for a meet. I may have an inkling who the perpetrator is. He *will* be reprimanded."

His word wasn't going to cut it with me. "Maybe we should—"

"Enough!" Drayton snapped, his eyes blazing down on me. He slowly turned his head to look at Dorian. "Thank you. Your assistance in this matter is very much appreciated. This will stay between us. I give you my word."

Dorian pinched the bridge of his nose, doing a great impression of someone stricken by remorse. "This is most embarrassing, highly irregular, but you have no idea how difficult the past two years have been for our kind. There will always be weak links in the chain, but please trust they will be purged."

Drayton smiled tightly. "And that is all we ask. Best of luck with the games." He gripped my hand, a sign that we should leave, but the doors behind us opened and a whirlwind of kicking and screaming was dragged into the room.

Dorian sat up straight, his eyes lighting up at the sight of the golden-haired female who was flinging every cuss word she could muster into the air.

"No. Let me go. I want to go home. Let me go!" She thrashed and bucked in Jeffery's arms.

I caught a glimpse of her face—the curve of her jaw and the arch of her brow. Jesse?

No, it wasn't my sister, just someone who

looked similar.

Jeffery, the butler, dropped her on the ground by Dorian, and she was on her feet in a second, her arm winding back to strike the lord.

"Stop!" Dorian's voice was a whiplash command.

The woman's hand halted an inch away from his face. "I fucking hate you. I hate you all. Let me go. I don't want to do this. This isn't what I signed up for. It isn't what any of us signed up for. You can't just keep us here."

"Enough."

Her hand dropped to her side. Dorian's thin lips curled in a cruel smile, and a moan rippled across the room, almost sexual in nature. Something was about to happen. The anticipation was a buzz in the air. Dorian turned the woman to face us, gently swiping her hair away from her neck. His tongue flicked out to moisten his lips, and his lips peeled back. There was something marring her creamy skin.

"Bite marks." My eyes widened.

Dorian's lips dropped over his fangs, hiding them from view. "Jeffery, you fool, you forgot the needle and drip."

Jeffery inclined his head and hurried from the room.

The woman's body trembled with impotent fury, and tears leaked from the corners of her eyes. Her body was locked in stasis by Dorian's command, but her gaze dragged to me. Rage and imploration mingled to stab at my heart. Fuck this shit.

"Let her go, Dorian." The words dropped from my lips like ice chips.

Dorian's jaw tensed. "Excuse me? You dare to order me?"

There it was, that primal edge that had been missing from this encounter all along, buried under a persona of civility—the lethal glint in his dark eyes, the pinprick of crimson that spoke of unbridled rage and insanity.

"This human belongs to my house. She belongs to me." His cultured tone had slipped into something guttural.

"Serenity," Drayton said. "He's right. She agreed to this. She signed a contract."

I rounded on him. "Agreed to being bitten? To being used as a walking fucking blood bag? You do see the bite marks, don't you?" I waved a hand toward the servers. "You do see what the fuck is happening here, don't you? Donating blood is one thing, but this ... This is fucking insane."

Drayton's jaw flexed. "I'm sure Dorian has addressed the oversight with regards to the biting."

The fuck was his problem? Why was he covering for this piece of shit?

Dorian inclined his head. "Of course."

The woman's eyes widened.

My pulse hammered in my throat with the

need to hurt someone. "How about you let her speak for herself?"

Dorian stepped away from the woman and padded toward me, a panther on the prowl.

Drayton took a step forward to shield me. "We're leaving. Now."

Dorian ignored him and kept his gaze fixed on me. "We bid for what we want here. We win and we get to reap. It's the way of Midnight. Everything is a gamble. I suggest you educate yourself on the ways of Midnight before you get hurt."

Drayton's control snapped. "Do not threaten her, Dorian."

Dorian blinked in surprise. "Or what, Drayton? You'll fuck me to death?"

The gathered broke into laughter — genuine this time — and Drayton bristled. His hands curled into fists. Shit. As much as I despised Dorian, as much as I wanted to punch his face in, we were in the lion's den. Two nephs surrounded by at least fifty or sixty Sanguinata.

It was my turn to grab Drayton's arm. "Let's jet."

We turned toward the door.

"Please!"

I spun to face the woman, who, by sheer force of will, had broken Dorian's compulsion. She fell to the ground, exhausted, her hand reaching for me. "Please don't leave me here with them."

She was someone's daughter, someone's sister. Somebody loved her just as I loved Jesse. I'd thought the winged were bad, but this ... This was something else. Rage bubbled up inside me, and my mouth developed a mind of its own.

I approached Dorian, not caring that he was a head and a half taller than me, that his fangs could tear me to shreds, or that we were in his territory at his mercy. Yeah, my mouth didn't give a shit about that. "You like to gamble, huh? Like to bid and play to win?"

Dorian cocked his head, intrigued. "You want to play, little neph?"

I licked my lips. What the heck was I doing? But the human's eyes had lit up with hope, and there was no going back now.

"Yeah, I want to play."

He crossed his arms. "I'm listening."

"Let me take part in your house games. I win, and every human gets the option to leave if they want."

"Serenity, no," Drayton cried.

A tray or something metallic clattered to the floor to my left. I kept my gaze on Dorian, my muscles vibrating with adrenaline. "Unless you're scared your big, bad Sanguinata players will lose to a girl." I batted my eyelashes. "I mean, they've already lost to the Lupin two years in a row. Maybe you're just not that good."

His lips twisted in amusement, and some

of my bravado evaporated. What did he have to be cocky about?

"Do you even know what the games are, little neph?" Dorian asked.

Shit. No one had filled me in on the details, but there was no way I was telling smug-arse that. "Of course I know what they are."

"Damn it, Serenity," Drayton snapped.

"Hush!" Dorian replied. "Let her speak. She has fire. I like that in a woman."

Ew. I crossed my arms under my breasts. "Do we have a deal?"

Dorian's lips peeled back, exposing lethal fangs. It wasn't a snarl, it was more of a … a come-on? "You have a deal, neph. But I have a condition of my own."

My mouth was suddenly dry as a subconscious part of my mind picked up on a threat I'd failed to consciously recognize. I shrugged, feigning nonchalance. "Go on."

He leaned in so his sweet, coppery breath wafted into my face. "If you lose, you give yourself to me."

"Serenity, no." Drayton yanked me toward him. "Stop this. Stop it now."

But I couldn't, not with all those eyes on me—the serving girls and boys with their hearts filled with the possibility of freedom.

I gently extricated my arm from Drayton's grasp and turned back to Dorian. "*If* I lose, you can do what you like with me. If I win, you let go of every human who wishes to leave, *and* you change the house recruitment contracts to allow future recruited humans to leave if they wish."

Dorian smiled smugly, and my hands itched to slap him.

Time to take a step away from temptation. "We have a deal?"

"Oh, yes, neph. We have a deal."

We left the castle, drove over the bridge, up the path, and out the gates in silence. All the while, the explosion was brewing. It crackled in the air and made my scalp prickle. Sure enough, once we were about half a mile away from the Sanguinata grounds, Drayton pulled up on the side of the road and turned off the engine.

"Drayton, I—"

"Fuck, fuck, fuck." Drayton slammed his hands against the wheel. His shoulders rose and fell in agitation.

"Drayton, chill. I can do this."

He turned on me. "Do what? What have you just signed up for? Have you any fucking idea? Huh?"

"It's a game. Like a test of skill or something."

He grabbed my shoulders and squeezed. "You stupid, impulsive fool. The games aren't a test of skill, they're a test of survival. They will hunt you, Serenity, and they will kill you."

Ice trickled down my spine. "Wait, no, that can't be right. He said if I lost then I'd be his, but if I lose, I'll be dead."

He released me and ran his hands over his face. "This is my fault. I should have spent more time filling you in, briefing you. If you'd been informed … It's my fault for being such a fucking moron about everything. If I hadn't avoided you …"

He was muttering to himself now, berating himself.

"Drayton, what the heck is going on?"

He sat back in his seat, his eyes on the empty stretch of road ahead. "If you lose, you die. But then Dorian will have you. He will raise you from the dead as one of his. You *will* belong to him."

"What? That makes no sense. I'd be dead."

"The Sanguinata can raise dead nephs and turn them into Sanguinata if the body is fresh enough. There is something in their blood, like a virus, an infection. They can't infect humans, but they can infect other nephs. But only when our bodies die, and it has to be pretty immediately after death." He shifted in his seat. "Do you see why you can't do this? You'll be up against seasoned Lupin and Sanguinata, killers trained to hunt. Trained specifically for the games." He grasped my hands in his. "They call them the killing games."

The killing games. I was meant to kill or be killed. Gooseflesh broke out over my skin, and I pulled my hands from his as my pulse spiked in fear. I was no assassin. Sure, I could hold my own against rippers and bloodsuckers, but so far we'd worked as a team. But solo, against Sanguinata and Lupin, in a bid to stay alive? I didn't have what it took.

"What if I just run and hide and stay alive until it's over?"

He pinched the bridge of his nose. "You could try, but the games span three days and two nights. They would find you. The object is to collect flags and kill your opponents. To win, you'd have to stay alive and collect more flags than the House of Vitae."

"Oh."

"Serenity, you don't have to do this. It's not like you signed a contract or anything."

No. There was no legal obligation, but those humans needed me. They needed me to help set them free.

I swallowed the lump of fear in my throat. "So, train me."

"What?" Drayton shook his head. "Serenity. No."

I looked up and met his gaze steadily. "I am *not* abandoning those humans. So, train me, and give me a shot at surviving."

He turned away, started the engine, and peeled away from the curb.

Shit.

"What did you do?" Bane crossed his arms over his chest and looked down his nose at me.

He was in standard Protectorate gear, just back from patrol if the mammoth sword strapped to his back was anything to go by. Shit, how did I always forget how big the guy was? Big and scary, and he wouldn't hurt me, not maliciously anyway. It didn't stop the cozy study from suddenly feeling dark and forbidding.

I took a deep breath. "I did what I had to do to help those humans. Isn't that what we do? Protect humans?"

He tucked in his chin. "Yes, Harker, that is what we do. But these humans made a conscious decision to accept the protection of House Vitae. They signed a contract. They receive protection for the blood they donate."

"Protection?" My voice rose an octave. "They're being treated like walking blood bags. Bitten, abused, and kept against their will. The Sanguinata are just as bad, if not worse, than the winged. At least the fuckers beyond the pearly gates are honest about the terms of the transaction. The Sanguinata lie."

Bane sighed and dropped his arms to his sides. "They don't lie. The contract is clear. It states that they must provide the Sanguinata with blood to the extent that it is not life-threatening to the human. If families sign up, they can rotate which adult donates for the whole family. Aside from the no biting clause, there is nothing to state how the blood will be extracted."

I didn't bother to hold back on the sarcasm. "So, it's the humans' fault that they fail to read between the lines?"

His violet eyes darkened. "This is the way of Midnight. It is a food chain, a balance that you must not interfere with. I know it seems barbaric to you, having been raised in Sunset, but this is how we live." He moved around the desk and leaned against it, his body a mere foot or so from mine. If I took a step, I'd be in his personal space. "If you mess with the balance, you force the hunter out of hiding. You lure the demon out from beneath the veneer of civility, and if that happens, then anarchy isn't far behind."

He had a valid point. Heck, what did I know about Midnight? But what was best wasn't always right.

"I understand what you're saying—"

"Good, then we'll forget all about it. Dorian will deal with the Sanguinata illegally recruiting, or he'll pretend to. Either way, he won't risk continuing. And we can move on to our next case." He picked up a file from the desk. "I'm going to let you run point on this one, with Drayton on hand to advise. See what you can do."

Damn it, he was dangling a carrot, and I was so ready to bite, but if I did that, if I went back on my word, the faces of those humans would haunt me forever. The blonde girl's face came to mind—her frightened eyes and her quivering hands. That could have been Jesse.

"I'm not backing down."

Bane's amiable expression tightened. He pushed off the desk and advanced into my personal space. "That is an order, Harker. Not a request." His voice was a warning rumble.

"You can't order me to *not* take part in the games. What I do in my free time is none of your business." Shit, I'd gone all squeaky again.

His lip curled, and fuck, there was that fang. "Free time? What free time? From now on, you have no free time. This case"—he shoved the file at me—"is your life. You will stop only to eat or sleep until you've put it to bed."

My mouth was like sandpaper. I licked my lips and he tracked the movement.

"You work for me. I own you. And don't even think about trying to quit, because that order I pushed through to allow your sister back to Sunset can just as easily be rescinded."

My eyes widened and my pulse raced. "You wouldn't."

"Try me."

My chest tightened with rage, and I grit my teeth. He was blackmailing me into backing down and leaving those humans to the Sanguinata's mercy.

"You're a cold-hearted bastard. You know that, Bane?"

He snorted. "Yeah, Harker. Born and fucking bred. Now get the fuck out of here and work that case." He turned away, dismissing me.

The file lay untouched on my bed while I paced the room, still fuming from my encounter with Bane. How dare he? How dare he blackmail me and order me about? Argh. Fuck him. I *was* taking part in those games whether he wanted me to or not. I'd find a way.

No, you won't.

"Oh, there you are. Decided to show up then, did you? Where were you with some dagger action and advice earlier?"

I'm sorry, Serenity. I would have been here if I could.

He sounded tired. "Are you all right?"

He chuckled. *I'm a voice in your head, what do you think?*

Had he just made a joke?

You can't take part in the games. If you do, you will fail.

"Wow, thanks for the vote of confidence."

Oh, I have confidence in you, Serenity. The problem is you don't have confidence in yourself.

"What the heck does that mean? I agreed to take part in the games, didn't I? That's pretty confident, as far as I'm concerned."

He sighed. *You doubt your abilities. You refuse to assimilate with the darkness.*

"That's because it's the *darkness*. The name kind of gives it away. It's my demon, and I'm in no hurry to give in to it. I've seen what the demon looks like. I saw Drayton's when it took over."

That was Drayton's demon, not yours. The demon is the other side of every nephilim, and the relationship between the two is unique to that pairing. It is often viewed as a separate entity, but it is not. They are simply two sides of the same coin. For too long now, the word has carried negative connotations, but did you know that in its original incarnation, the word "daimon" meant a divine power, a guiding spirit, a tutelary force?

"No. I didn't."

No, you think only of evil and harm. Drayton's daimon takes over and feeds to protect him, to ensure his survival. It is singular in its goal. Nephilims' daimons are a gift from your Black Wing ancestors, and they wish you no harm, because to do so would be wishing harm on themselves. Your darkness is your demon. It's a part of you. And until you recognize that, you will never be whole.

His words resonated inside me. But my shields had been my crutch for too long. He'd proven that the darkness would listen even without the shields, and that I didn't really need the walls, but it was one thing jumping off a cliff when you were high with craving and another to do it stone-cold sober.

You know I'm right.

My stomach squirmed.

Do you ever wonder how the daggers know when to materialize?

"Um, you tell them?"

He snorted. You *tell them, or at least the subconscious part of you does. The part that is primed to protect you. The darkness. Your demon.*

No...

The daggers are connected to it, and once you let it in, once you accept it, you will have control of the daggers.

All my life, the hunger had been a separate entity. Or had it? I'd certainly treated it as a separate entity. Had I made this happen? But then how else would I have coped in a district of humans?

It's time to make some changes.

"I know, but—"

A knock on the door interrupted my flow. Crap. "Come in."

Ambrosius retreated back to wherever he came from.

Drayton stepped into the room. "Bane said he gave you a file?"

I crossed my arms and glared at him. "Tattle-tale."

He rolled his eyes. "It's called protocol."

"No. It's called being a snitch."

He pressed his lips together. "The file?"

He obviously wasn't going to bite. I waved a hand toward the paperwork on my desk. "I thought the MPD didn't do paperwork."

"We don't. Not unless it's passed to us by the MED." He stepped farther into the room. "What is it?"

"I haven't looked yet."

He arched a brow. "Really?"

His tone said it all. He knew I was still stinging from Bane's reprimand, but he was surprised I hadn't devoured the contents of the file — my first official case. He picked up the file and flipped it open.

"Oh, shit." He held it out to me.

"What?" I took it and stared at the familiar arrogant face glaring back at me from the photograph pinned inside. It was the kelpie guy from The Deep. Cassie's ex, Killion. In all the hullabaloo, we'd completely forgotten to ask her about his man-eating ways, but it looked like he'd been up to his tricks again.

A partially devoured body had been located in the south cove, and it wasn't the first time, according to the file. But although Killion was a suspect, the evidence was circumstantial at best. He'd been seen speaking to the victim earlier that evening. Spotted in the vicinity where the body was found, that kind of thing.

The MED wanted us to investigate, to gather evidence, prints, and teeth impressions, things the MED wouldn't be able to obtain. They wanted us to put a stop to the killings.

I closed the file and handed it back to Drayton.

"So, you're running point on this one," he said. "What's our first call?"

I grabbed my jacket off the end of the bed. "First, we talk to Cassie."

His face sobered. "I was hoping you wouldn't say that."

Cassie crossed her arms under her breasts, her chin jutting out in defiance. "Killion didn't do it."

We were in her pink, perfumed boudoir filled with fluffy pillows. She'd just stepped out of the shower, hair still wet. Her body was wrapped in a bathrobe, and her pink toenailed foot tapped on the carpet in agitation.

I sighed. "Cassie, I heard you talking about it at The Deep. It's why you told me to take a walk."

Her lips turned down. "You're mistaken."

She was covering for a human killer. My patience snapped. "I know what I heard. You can either talk to us or explain to Bane why you're covering for a man-eater?"

She averted her gaze. "He's a good guy. He does his best to fight his nature, but sometimes it's too much. Can you imagine fighting who you are every single day?"

I snorted. "Yes, I can, actually, and it's fucking hard, but not impossible." I shoved the file at her. "Look at it, look at what his loss of control did."

She made a sound of exasperation in the back of her throat but took the file, opening it reluctantly to scan the awfully graphic photos. She blinked at the pictures, then glanced up at Drayton. "Why has Harker got this file?"

"Bane has Serenity running point on this one," Drayton explained.

She made an 'o' with her mouth, then closed it quickly. "He didn't do this. This wasn't him."

"How can you be so sure?"

"Because he *swore* he wouldn't. That night at The Deep, he swore to me that it would never happen again."

Oh, man. This woman was delusional.

"Cassie," Drayton said. "It was found in the south cove, the entrance and exit to Killion's sea riders' harras domain."

"So, it could be one of the others. It's not him," she insisted.

I tapped the file against my thigh. "Is a harras like a pack?"

"Yes," Drayton confirmed.

So, the kelpies had their little groups too then. Interesting. "Fine, Cassie. Help us prove him innocent. Come with us. Get him to talk to us and give us the evidence we need to clear him."

She pressed her lips together. "Fine. I'll meet you in the foyer in fifteen minutes."

We left her to get dressed and made our way downstairs. "What if she's right? What if he didn't do it?"

Drayton shrugged. "Then we find whoever did. We solve the case before another human gets eaten. That's what we do."

"Could it be The Breed?"

His body tensed. "No. They wouldn't encroach on kelpie territory. Besides, they're not known for leaving any evidence behind. If The Breed does get hold of you, then you simply go missing. There are very few exceptions to that rule." He sounded bitter.

"And no one has brought them to justice?"

"We'd have to find them first. The fuckers are ghosts. They come and go as they please. Sometimes, I wonder if they're nephs or something else."

"I thought everything supernatural was a neph of some kind? That they all had Black Wing blood."

"Yes, so did I. But the sea dwellers are rumored to be descended from Black Wing blood and the blood of an ancient race that wasn't human. Who knows what The Breed really is?"

His voice was thick with emotion. He had a

score to settle with The Breed; they'd hurt him somehow.

I touched his arm lightly. "What did they do to you?"

He faltered going down the steps, and for a moment, I thought he was going to open up and tell me, but then he took the rest of the stairs at a trot, eager to get away from me.

Cassie joined us a few minutes later, a black case clutched in her hands. "Print and mold kit for evidence. Thought you might need it." She smiled, her previous anxiety gone. "Now, let's crack this case."

The south cove was bordered by sand dunes and chalky rock. Leaving the car parked up on the main track, we picked our way down to the beach. The sea here was filled with jagged rocks that poked up like dark fingers reaching for the sky.

Okay, so we were here, what now? I hated that I didn't have a clue what I was actually doing here. "How do we call Killion?"

Cassie picked up a smooth pebble, wound her arm back, and launched it into the sea. She waited a moment, picked up another, and threw that one in too. Drayton joined her in the pebble throwing. Was this the equivalent of knocking on their door?

The water began to ripple, and Cassie and

Drayton quickly backed up the beach. A massive form rose out of the water, silver and black, with a mane of twisted, blackened seaweed. It tossed its head and then began to cut through the water toward shore. It was a horse, a terrifying seahorse with mist curling from its nostrils and pluming out behind it, and then it wasn't. It was a man. A large, powerfully built male, dry as bone and standing at the water's edge. His lower body was encased in dark pants, and he was sporting some pretty expensive-looking boots. A white shirt clung to his muscles, accentuating every dip and ripple. He raked us over with an intense gaze that finally came to rest on Cassie.

"What do you want?" he asked.

Cassie smiled, but it was a perfunctory action. "Hello, Finlay. It's good to see you too. Where's Killion?"

Finlay frowned. "Not here." He shrugged. "I'll tell him you dropped by." He turned to leave.

I took a step toward the water. "Whoa, wait up a second."

He glanced over his shoulder, his dark eyes gleaming in the moonlight. "I have business to attend to."

"Yeah? And we didn't come down here for a romantic stroll."

His lips twitched and he turned to face me. "You have two minutes."

I handed him the file. "Is this the work of

one of your people ... maybe even your brother?"

Finlay let out a bark of laughter. "Blunt and to the point. Finally, someone who doesn't fuck around." He scanned the photographs, his lip curling in disgust. "No kelpie would ever feed in this way. It's messy and out of control. When we devour, our prey does not struggle, they are consumed in ecstasy."

"Ecstasy? I doubt being eaten is in any way pleasant."

"Finlay, what do you mean?" Drayton asked.

"Digging for more information on our kind, are you, incubus? Are you going to add it to the file your siren keeps?"

Drayton sighed. "We just want to catch whoever is doing this and put a stop to it."

Finlay handed the file back to me. "Kelpies secrete a pheromone that puts the humans into a state of bliss. They feel nothing while we feed."

"Nothing?"

"Nothing."

He smiled, showcasing neat white teeth. They flashed to razor-sharp then back to blunt, reminding me that he may look like a guy, but he was something entirely different. "In the old days, when we were permitted to hunt and feed as required, a human would last for days, suspended in a state of bliss while we fed on him bit by bit. We kept stores, and we were never hungry. Now, we are forced to live off fish and algae, to eat human food and pollute our bodies." He snorted. "Predators were born to hunt, but we're denied that right, because the precious human sheep must be protected at all costs."

"Well, if you have nothing to hide, then you wouldn't mind giving us some prints and allowing us to take a mold of your teeth. Your real teeth."

His brows shot up, and he looked to Drayton. "Is she insane?" He turned away. "Get out of my territory. I'm done talking. I have important shit to do."

"Finlay!" a male voice called out.

We looked up the beach to see two kelpies jogging toward us.

"We searched the east coast and—"

"Enough," Finlay snapped. "We have guests. Guests who are about to leave."

My gut twinged. "What were they searching for?"

The corner of Finlay's mouth turned up. "I'm done answering your questions. But I'd be happy to continue with some pillow talk." He cocked his head. "Always wondered what it'd be like to fuck one of the Protectorate." His gaze slid to Cassie. "Killion swears by it."

"Thanks, but I'll pass."

The other kelpies had joined us, and Finlay led them back into the water. They got hip deep before their bodies morphed and twisted into equine form, and then they dove under and were gone.

"Did you know about the bliss thing?" Drayton asked Cassie.

"No. Killion and I ... we didn't really spend a huge amount of time talking." She blushed.

I gnawed on my bottom lip, focusing on my gut, on what my instincts were telling me. They were clearer with the shields down a fraction. Maybe the voice was right. "I think Finlay was telling the truth about the bliss, and about Killion not being involved, but he is hiding something." I turned and headed up the beach. "And I think we need to search the east coast."

Cassie grabbed my arm. "East coast is off limits. It's rival pack territory owned by the Ocean Hunter harras. Juno's gang. That bitch is vicious."

I arched a brow. "And yet Killion's guys were just there searching. We need to figure out what they were looking for."

"Why?" Cassie looked genuinely perplexed.

"Because my gut tells me to, okay. Look, Bane put me in charge, so we go to the east coast." I marched up the dunes toward the road and the parked car. "Um, now if one of you will just drive me there?"

Cassie joined me at the car. "Fine. Juno's pack is probably deep under sea at the moment anyway, otherwise Killion's guys wouldn't have risked a sweep of her land."

"Well, it would be worth questioning her,

right?" I looked to Drayton.

"Juno doesn't do questions." He unlocked the car. "If Juno and her cronies show up, we make our apologies and leave."

Man, he was getting on my nerves with all the bowing out—first with Dorian and now Juno. It was as if he didn't want to get to the bottom of the case. We were meant to be law enforcers, protectors of Midnight, and if we didn't ask questions and rattle a few cages, then how the heck were we going to get any answers?

"If Juno shows up, we question her." My tone was firm, brooking no argument. I opened the passenger door. "Bane gave me a case. He trusted me to do a good job, and I don't intend to cut corners and let him down."

Cassie and Drayton exchanged glances.

"What?" They were looking at me strangely, almost pityingly.

"Seriously, what the heck is going on?"

"Serenity, you—"

"She's right." Drayton cut Cassie off. "We need to be thorough."

Cassie snapped her mouth closed and climbed into the car. There was my gut again, telling me they were both hiding something. But I had a case to solve and some sand to examine. Yay, me.

The east coast stretch of sand was wider,

bordered by strange leafy plants that swayed in the breeze. Shells and seaweed were strewn close to the water's edge, and the ocean was a calm slate. Far in the distance, a tiny island rose up, black against the midnight sky.

"What's that?" I pointed out to sea.

"It's Desert Rock," Drayton said. "The sea dwellers use it to sunbathe and sometimes hold parties. It's barren, though—no vegetation. Just a huge, rocky island."

We began to search the sands, looking for anything odd or out of the ordinary. Killion's guys had said they'd searched but not what they'd found, if anything. This was probably a pointless exercise, but ignoring my gut instincts wasn't an option.

While Cassie and Drayton moved off down the beach, I headed over to the weird grass and began poking around. The sand here was earthy as it transitioned into soil, and pressed into it neatly—almost as if it were deliberate—was an animal footprint.

"Drayton, Cassie, over here!" I signaled by waving my arms, then bent to examine the print. There was another and another—a trail leading away from the beach.

"What is it?"

"Tracks. Can you tell what made them?"

Drayton crouched to examine the prints. "Ripper."

"I thought this was kelpie territory? Would

a ripper come here?"

Cassie exhaled through her nose. "No. Rippers may come across as mindless killing machines, but they have predatory instincts, and they know when to steer clear of another predator's territory."

"Shame they don't consider humans predators."

"Humans have become domesticated," Drayton said. "They no longer use their predator instincts, and other predators can pick up on that, they can smell it. Humans are, and always will be, prey."

He had a point. "Question is, what were Killion's guys looking for, and did they find it? Was this what they found?"

Once again, Drayton and Cassie exchanged a look that had my scalp prickling. I stood up. "Spill it. If it's to do with this case, I need to know."

Drayton pressed his hands to his thighs and pushed himself up. "It's not important."

"Damn it, Dray. It so is," Cassie said.

"Cassie..." Drayton warned.

Cassie ignored him. "Look, after you came to me with that file, I spoke to Bane, because I recognized the photographs. The case isn't even recent, Harker. It's an MED cold case. He asked them to send it over to distract you from this whole house games thing."

"A cold case?"

"At least six months old. They never figured out who did it, because the body was too mangled. It got shelved. There were no others like it. They couldn't even identify the human."

Bane had given me a dud case to keep me sweet. The fire in my limbs died a little. No. Fuck that. "It may be a cold case, but it's still a case. This human still died, and I'm going to find out who killed him."

"We have company," Drayton said.

I tracked his gaze to see several shapes moving toward us through the water. Wiry, slender, and inhuman, their skin was dark with a silver sheen that melted away to reveal human skin. It was a trick, a glamour that turned the terrifying carnivorous seahorse into a perky-breasted beauty with golden waves. She wasn't able to hide the truth behind her eyes, though. They remained dark, radiating power and knowledge.

She was old. Ancient.

"Hello, Juno," Drayton said amiably. "Fancy seeing you here."

Juno blinked slowly at him. "I feel it is I who should be saying this to you. What are you doing here, incubus? This is my domain. There is no unlawful activity here."

"No," Cassie said. "Just some ripper activity."

Her eyes narrowed. "Rippers? You saw them?"

"Tracks." I pointed at the ground. "Several of them."

Her nostrils flared and her face rippled as she battled with her emotions.

"Juno, should we sweep?" one of her companions asked.

She nodded curtly. "Go, both of you. If you find them, end them. It will teach them to come back this way again."

Again? "The rippers have been here before?"

Juno looked at me. "Rippers have been acting strange. Testing boundaries." She sniffed the air, and her lips curled. "It seems others have been testing boundaries too." Her eyes were slits, as if she was considering doing someone bodily harm.

I held out the file. "Can you take a look at this? Maybe tell me what you think may have done this."

Drayton tensed. He'd warned me about questioning her.

And she was looking at me as if considering which limb to start with when dismembering me.

I smiled warmly. "I know you're probably really busy, running a harras and all, but it would mean so much if you could spare the time to help a girl out." I shrugged. "The boss blatantly thinks I can't close this case."

The corner of her mouth twitched, and she

held out her hand for the file. Her slender, pale fingers were a little bit too long.

I handed it to her and inclined my head. "Much appreciated."

She had a quick look, then shrugged. "It is too mangled to tell." She met my eyes. "It is not a kelpie, if that is what you think." She tapped the photo of Killion. "Certainly not him. This is an MED file, correct?"

"Yes."

"The humans are pathetic. They have no clue. If we were to feed, there would be no evidence left to find."

"Then how has Killion gotten on their radar?"

"*Pfft*, Killion has a big mouth. He likes to brag, and people listen. His words get passed on."

Made sense, especially with what Finlay had said about the pheromone. It looked like we'd have to reassess our strategy. I accepted the file back.

"You're wasting your time, and mine." Her tone was suddenly cold and curt. She dismissed us, turning to the ocean. "Get off my land. I have better things to do with my time."

Which was exactly what Finlay had said.

"What kind of better things?" The words were out before I could stop them.

She turned slowly to face me and pushed her hair out of her face. "That is none of your damned business."

"Where did you get that?" Cassie barreled forward and grabbed Juno's wrist.

The kelpie stared at her in surprise. "What? This?" It was a necklace of colorful beads wound around her wrist several times.

"Yes. Where did you get it?" Cassie insisted.

Juno shrugged. "I found it washed up on Desert Rock."

"It belongs to Killion. I made it for him. He wears it always."

Juno pulled her wrist away. "Well, it's mine now. He should have taken better care of it."

The other kelpies she'd sent off to do a sweep of her territory for rippers returned clutching something that looked like a scarf. The blue and yellow fabric was torn, and the kelpie male held it out to his leader.

Juno took it from him with trembling fingers.

"Is it his?" the male kelpie asked.

Juno nodded. "Yes. It's Leo's."

"I picked up south coast harras scent," the male said.

Juno's jaw tightened, and her eyes flashed. "Yes. So did I. So did I." She glanced our way. "If you know what's good for you, I suggest you steer clear of the coves for the next few days. Just a friendly warning."

They bounded toward the ocean and were gone too quickly, slipping beneath the waves.

I looked to Cassie. "Who's Leo?"

"Juno's mate. I was surprised he wasn't with her," Cassie said.

"She looked upset ... scared."

Cassie pressed her lips together. "Something is wrong. We need to go back and speak to Killion."

"I agree there's definitely something going on between the kelpie gangs, but it doesn't pertain to our case."

Cassie's jaw tensed. "The case can go jump. If something's wrong with Killion, if shit is about to go down, then I need to know."

I sighed. "Fine, let's pay Finlay another visit."

Drayton's phone buzzed. "Hello?" He started walking toward the car.

Cassie and I followed and reached Drayton just as he hung up the phone. "There's trouble at the fete. Order of Merlin. Ryker and Orin are on their way, but the event is huge, so we need to go in as backup."

A fete? They were having a fete?

"It's MED jurisdiction," Cassie snapped, clearly annoyed it was taking us away from the kelpie intrigue. She growled in exasperation. "Look, just drop me off up the road. I'll speak to Finlay then meet you at the fete."

She really cared about this Killion guy.

Poor Orin.

Drayton nodded, and we piled into the ride. A fete in Midnight? Now this I had to see.

"The fete is an annual event," Drayton said as we drove across the district. "It's humans only, armed MED operatives at the gates, the works. It's meant to be a safe event. We've never had any issues before."

"The Order's never tried to recruit there?"

"No. Never."

"Weird. Why start now?"

"Who knows why The Order does what it does. They're a fanatical sect." He was silent for a long beat. "I'm sorry about the case. I didn't know Bane would do that."

"But you knew what he'd done when you saw the file."

"Yes."

"And you pretended."

"Like you said, it's still a case."

God, he was so infuriating. "Dammit, Drayton. If you're going to be all weird with me after what happened in the basement, then we shouldn't work together."

He exhaled sharply. "I'm sorry."

Gosh, none of this was his fault. It was mine. "No. I am. If I hadn't left you underground, then you wouldn't have been taken by the sentinel and forced to use up all your power. Your demon would never have taken control."

He shot me a surprised look. "Is that what you think? Damn it, Harker. If you'd stayed, you would have been cocooned too. We'd have died, as no one would have come to help us."

Okay, he had a point, but still, that feeling that I could have done more wouldn't be shaken.

"There was nothing more you could have done, and I'm grateful for everything you did. It's just … I could have killed you."

"It was worth the risk." The words slipped from my mouth, soft and filled with meaning.

His hands clenched on the wheel. "Serenity…"

There was so much longing in that one word it made my heart ache, and that wasn't a direction that would yield any positive results. It was time to focus on the here and now. On the case.

I cleared my throat. "Of course I'm disappointed Bane only gave me this case to distract me. But it's still a case, and you need to understand that I meant what I said to Dorian.

Instead of fighting me on this, you need to help me prepare. I can't back down on this and live with myself, do you understand?"

Drayton was silent for a long time, probably adjusting the switchback in topic, and then he sighed. "I understand, but you need to understand that we can't let you do this. Bane must have explained."

"Yeah, he said his piece." Biding my time was kinda my thing, and there was no point arguing with Bane right now. I'd wear them down eventually. At least Drayton seemed to have relaxed around me again. His body wasn't in fight or flee mode any longer, the tension had ebbed, and he was at ease again. There was something ultimately satisfying about being forthright.

"Here we go," he said.

Twinkling lights came into view, accompanied by music that bordered somewhere between creepy and cheery. The entrance to the green where the fete was being held was wrapped in huge multicolored bulbs that flashed on and off, and an impromptu fence had been rigged up. The fete car park was rammed with cars, but Drayton pulled up right next to the entrance. We got out and jogged under the pretty arch and dove right into the hustle and bustle of the fete. The scent of barbecued food hit me hard, and my chest cramped in nostalgia. Not long ago, I'd been at a fete of my own. A Sunset fete with Jesse and her wonderful cakes. We'd never had a chance to enjoy that day, and we never would.

Drayton came to a standstill and searched the crowd of humans holding hands and kids tucked up against maternal thighs or hoisted high on paternal shoulders. This was good, wholesome fun in a place of darkness and terror, and it warmed my twisted little heart to see it.

"There he is," Drayton said. He raised a hand. "Hey, Langley!"

Langley spotted us and strode over. "They're by the Ferris wheel. A whole group of them."

The wheel was clearly visible as the largest attraction at the fete, its twinkling lights a beacon to all. The last time we'd crossed paths with The Order, they'd tried to kill us. Adrenaline pumping, I followed Drayton as he cut a path through the revelers — people perfectly at ease, milling about and enjoying the fete until we started barging through.

"Dray! Harker." Ryker came running toward us from the left, Orin in tow. "The wheel," he said.

Drayton nodded. "Yeah, on our way."

We made it to the attraction, where a crowd had gathered. A man dressed in everyday clothes stood on a raised platform, his hands up with the palms out as he addressed the crowd. "Join us and be free, join us and be liberated.

Together, we can break down the barriers and enter the real world. There is more to life than Midnight, more than Arcadia. Come with us and be enlightened. Come with us, and, together, we can be free."

The crowd was silent, enraptured by his words.

"What the fuck?" Ryker said. "Look at them. They're lapping up this crap." He scanned the gathered. "Where's the riot?"

"Well, what are you waiting for?" Langley appeared with a couple of MED officials. "Get rid of them."

Ryker stared down his nose at the officer. "I thought you said this was a *situation*." He looked back at the crowd. "Looks pretty peaceful to me."

"They aren't supposed to be here," Langley insisted. "Humans only, remember."

"Then ask them to leave," Drayton said. "You don't need us, unless shit gets out of hand."

Langley smirked. "Oh, but I do. The Order is supernatural, and supernatural is *your* jurisdiction, remember." His smile widened. "So, clean it up."

This was payback for the missing person case we'd taken off him. He'd called us all the way here just to ask The Order to vacate the premises. The fucker was getting us back for stealing his case by wasting our time.

Ryker took a threatening step toward Langley, but Orin grabbed his arm. "Leave it. He's not worth it, not to mention you'd probably end up breaking his face."

Langley's smile slipped, and he took a step back.

Orin huffed and pushed through the crowd of humans. "Hey. Order dude."

The Order representative paused in his speech.

"You need to leave."

The Order member inclined his head. "Of course. I was merely spreading the word, and if any should wish to join me?"

A murmur rose up in the crowd.

The guy smiled and stepped off his platform, then picked it up and began to walk off. There was a second of stunned silence, and then a bunch of humans followed.

Orin turned to us, his eyes wide. He shook his head in a what-the-heck gesture.

"They're going with him," Drayton said. "Looks like the humans of Midnight are beginning to slip."

Langley shook his head in disgust and strode off into the crowd.

Ryker's lip curled. "We're done here."

Bane paced the lounge floor. Langley's little power play had him fuming, but Ryker and

Drayton had done all the cursing for him.

"I'll set up a meeting with the MED," Bane said. "Smooth this over and press reset. If we're going to keep Midnight safe, then we can't have this kind of petty rivalry. Our resources were abused today. They pulled you off an actual case when they could have dealt with The Order themselves."

He didn't know I was aware he'd given me a cold case, and now wasn't the time to bring it up, but he'd hear my views on his tactics soon enough—once I'd solved the case.

Orin and Rivers were out on patrol, and Ryker was taking a power nap before he had to head out with Cassie.

"Where is Cassie?" Bane asked, as if reading my thoughts.

Drayton filled him in on our conversation with the kelpie gangs.

Bane's brow furrowed. "If something is up, if there is going to be conflict between them, then we need to shut down the coast for a while to protect the humans. Maybe speak to Jonah and ask him to warn the patrons."

The clip of Cassie's boots had us all looking toward the door. She appeared a moment later, cheeks flushed and eyes bright.

"I was right. There is something wrong." She headed over to the drinks tray and poured herself a brandy, downed it, and then poured another.

"Cassie?" Bane walked up to her and placed a hand on her back. "Talk to me."

She shook her head and sniffed. "Killion is missing." She tilted her face up to Bane. "He's been missing for almost a week, and two more went missing a couple of days ago."

And they'd been searching Juno's territory. "They think ocean hunters are responsible, don't they?"

Cassie nodded. "I told Finlay we spoke to Juno and how weird she was when they found Leo's scarf."

"You think Leo's missing too?"

She nodded. "They're going to meet in a few hours, and then, hopefully, things will be clearer."

Whoever is taking the kelpies was probably banking on the gangs blaming each other. "Who'd want to kidnap kelpies?"

Bane shrugged a massive shoulder. "Midnight is becoming more and more unpredictable. We need to be prepared for anything. Where are the kelpies meeting?"

"The Deep. It's neutral ground."

"Good. Drayton and Harker will go to the meeting, find out what's happening, and offer our assistance."

"What about me? I need to be there."

Bane's expression smoothed out. "No. You're too emotionally invested."

She wiped at her eyes. "I'm not. I can do

this. I need to be there."

"I've made my decision. This isn't your case."

Her lips twisted. "Oh, are you going to give me a dud case just to distract me like you did for Harker?"

Bane's eyes narrowed and his lips thinned. "I'm going to let that slide because I know you're upset. But one is all you get, Cassie."

Cassie's mouth trembled. "If anything happens to him…"

Damn, she really cared about her ex. No, it was more than care. She was in love with him.

Bane sighed. "Go get cleaned up. We'll keep you updated."

She wiped her nose on her sleeve, drained her glass, and then left the room.

Bane met my gaze. "You have something you want to say to me, then get it off your chest now."

He was referring to Cassie letting the cat out of the bag about the cold case. God, I had so much to say, but he held all the cards. If I wanted to keep Jesse safe and help the humans locked into contract with the Sanguinata, I needed to get on his good side and prove myself to him.

"I've got nothing to say."

"Good. Now come here; you need to feed and rest before you go to The Deep."

"She can feed on Rivers," Drayton said

tightly.

"Rivers isn't here. She'll feed on me, and it will sustain her for longer."

Rivers had allowed me to siphon off him after I'd tapped out fighting Arachne, but Bane was right, I needed a top-up. And hadn't Ambrosius made a fuss about me staying on top of my hunger and not starving my demon? But Drayton's closed expression, his tense shoulders and the way he refused to look anywhere else but at me, left a nauseous feeling in the pit of my stomach. I pushed myself off the sofa and walked over to Bane.

"If you're going to shove your tongue down her throat, then do it in private," Drayton said tightly.

Bane snorted. "She doesn't need sexual energy. Not this time." He ran his violet gaze over my face, lingering on my lips and the base of my neck, where my pulse was going haywire for some inexplicable reason. "Do you?"

I swallowed past the lump in my throat and shook my head. "No. I'm good. That was a one-off."

"To save your arse, you ungrateful arsehole," Bane snapped.

Drayton stood. "I know, and I appreciate it. She knows that."

I glanced his way, but he was already walking out the door.

"He will be fine," Bane said. "Drayton is no

stranger to heartache and yearning. None of us are."

Was he talking about Drayton and me? And what was Bane's heartache? Who did he yearn for?

Bane rolled up his sleeve, exposing a thick, taut forearm corded with muscle. "Take what you need. *Satisfy* yourself."

I slid my hands over his arm and completely dropped my shields. I closed my eyes as my darkness rose, ready to feed, but he pinched my chin with his free hand and jerked it up.

"Look at me." His voice was rough. "Look at me when you take from me."

His pupils were a hungry abyss filled with starlight, and while my conscious mind floated in their depths, my demon slammed into him, latching on and siphoning. A moan fell from his lips, and his hand slid from my chin to cup my face and then the back of my neck, while his calloused thumb ran up and down my cheek, sending delicious shivers along my spine. His honey power flowed into me, thick and invigorating. I needed more, needed to feel more. I needed to slide my hands under his shirt and over his chest, to rest just above his heart and feel the power of every steady beat. I wanted to lick the corded column of his neck and revel in the erratic beat of his pulse against my tongue.

"Serenity..." My name was said in wonder, as if it was a revelation.

He knew. He knew my thoughts and my demon's thoughts. The heat of embarrassment climbed up my neck and settled on my cheeks. I broke contact and stepped out of his grasp.

The world was bright for a second, and then the familiar lethargy that came after a feeding with him seeped into my limbs, and the world dimmed.

"I have you, Harker. I have you."

I woke in my room, on my bed, fresh and rejuvenated. Was it time to go yet? How long had I been out? Surely Drayton would have come to find me if it was time to go. The thought of the incubus had black butterflies hatching in my stomach. He'd been jealous of Bane, of the fact I'd collected sexual energy from him. Was that another reason Drayton had been cool and distant toward me? Not just the fact that I'd seen his demon, or that he'd almost killed me. There was nothing I could do about that, but maybe there was something I could do to address his *softly, softly* approach when it came to the kelpies and the House of Vitae. If we were going to be working together, his overly cautious attitude had to go, because he was giving them power with his acquiescence.

A knock interrupted my thoughts.

I swung my legs off the bed. "Come in."

Drayton slipped into my room and stood awkwardly by the door. "It's about time we left."

I pulled on my boots. "Yeah. Let's. This is what we do, right? Keep the supernatural side of Midnight in check?"

"Of course." His tone was wary.

He'd picked up on my undertone. Sod it, best to just go in for the kill. "Look, can you just promise me one thing this time?"

"What?"

"That you won't allow them to push us out of the discussion. If kelpies are being taken, then we need to be involved in getting them back."

His brows dropped low over his eyes. "Is that what you think? That I get strong-armed and pushed around?"

Shit. "No. I didn't say that. You just have this softly, softly approach. Like with the House of Vitae, and then again when I suggested speaking to Juno."

He held up a hand. "You may think barging in and demanding answers is the best form of action, and, heck, it may have worked for you in Sunset. But here, in Midnight, things are different."

"I get that, but—"

"I haven't finished." His expression was stern. "On both occasions, we were on another neph's turf, *their* territory, and, yes, we were investigating a case, but that does *not* mean we can abandon all etiquette. The Sanguinata are respected members of Midnight's society. And the kelpies, as far as we're aware, have caused no harm. By all means, we must continue with our enquiries, but we don't need to be rude about it."

When he put it that way, it was hard not to see his point. He must have read my thoughts on my face because his expression softened. He stepped into the room and held out his hand to me. I allowed him to tug me up.

"There is a balance to this world," he said softly. "One day, you might understand. Humanity is important, but you can't blame the tiger for hunting deer, just like you can't blame the kelpie for craving human flesh or the Sanguinata for hungering for blood."

"I get it. But humans aren't deer. We can't just let them be consumed. I can't just stand by and allow the Sanguinata to hold their donors hostage like that."

His chest rose and fell in a sigh as he pulled me closer. "Midnight is a mess. Arcadia is a mess. This isn't how things are supposed to be."

"Then how are they supposed to be?" Did he know something? Did he know about the outside? "What do you know? Tell me."

He reached up to caress my face. "Trust me, Serenity. Sometimes it's best not to know what you're missing. That way you can't crave it."

Oh, God. He was looking at me in that way again—the one that made my knees weak and my pulse race. Was he talking about Arcadia or us?

"One day, you'll understand. One day, it will all make sense. And all this will have been worth it. One day, you'll know why you're here."

"Do *you* know why I'm here?" The words came out breathless and whispery.

He smiled and shook his head. "No, but I know there's a reason." His gaze was a caress wandering across my face. "There has to be. I don't believe in chance and coincidence. I believe in tests and orchestrated maneuvers. I believe that you're here because you have a purpose."

What was he trying to tell me? "So, how do *we* fit into that? You and me. If it's not chance and not coincidence, then what is this?" I reached up to stroke his chin. Bold move, but fuck it, I was in a bold kinda mood.

His eyes fluttered closed and his face tightened as if he was in pain. "There can be no us, and that, Harker, is a cruel twist of fate." He released me and stepped away. "We should go."

When he looked at me now, his beautiful brown eyes were guarded, and my chest ached with a loss that made no sense, because I'd never had anything to lose in the first place.

The drive to The Deep was a silent one, which was fine by me. It was time to reflect and get my head in order for the kelpie showdown. No doubt sparks would fly when the two harrases got together.

The building was as busy as the last time we'd visited, but there was no sign of the kelpies yet. Drayton sidled up to the bar and had a quick word with Jonah. It was impossible to hear what they were saying, so I did a quick survey of the dance floor. Like the last time, it was packed with bodies moving in sync. Laughter and harmony in a twisted landscape. The Deep really was a haven for neph and human unions, because now that I studied it closely, there were more than a few mixed couples on the dance floor. The crowd parted for a second, and my gaze skimmed over a tall guy wearing a black turtleneck sweater. He lounged against a pillar, drink clutched casually in his hand. He was alone and people-watching just like me. Our gazes locked for a second, and he raised his glass in a silent greeting. Then the crowd shifted, and he was gone.

"They're not here yet." Drayton's breath tickled my ear.

Damn him and his scent. "So, what shall we do? Wait in the car?"

Drayton's gaze slipped over my head and onto the main floor, where a slow, crooning number was playing. The corner of his mouth turned up almost wistfully.

He slipped his hand into mine. "We *could* dance?"

Butterflies bloomed in my chest. He'd said there would be no us, that there could never be an us, so why was he looking at me like that? "Dance?"

His smile widened. "Yes, you know that thing where you shuffle from side to side to the music."

My misgivings melted and I grinned. "Well, if that's the only move you have, then I think I'll pass."

He leaned in. "Oh, honey. You have no idea what moves I have."

My pulse fluttered. What was he playing at? And why was I considering playing along? "Well, in that case, you'll just have to demonstrate."

We slipped onto the dance floor and he pulled me against him. My body pressed flush against his for the first time. We'd kissed twice, but both times it had been to feed. This ... this contact was intimate and spine-melting. His hand came to rest on the base of my spine, fingers splayed. I tilted my chin to look up into his face, and my heart climbed into my throat and sat there, beating wildly, because in that moment there was no barrier, just uncensored, unbridled adoration. This wasn't desire, this ...

Oh, God. He closed his eyes, exhaled through his nostrils, and tucked in his chin to press his forehead to mine.

We swayed to the love song, shuffling from side to side just like he'd predicted, and I finally understood why this move worked. It was perfect.

The track changed, and the spell was broken. Drayton gently pulled back and extricated himself from me.

His throat bobbed, and he tore his gaze away and looked over my head. "The sea riders just walked in."

It was time to get down to business.

Looked like the gangs had hired a private room, and Jonah wasn't too happy about letting us back there. But Drayton played the MPD card and Jonah caved. We slipped into the room-for-hire, and the noise hit me first. Curses and threats and accusations were being traded. Sea riders faced off with ocean hunters — Juno with her four henchmen and Finlay and his backup. It was about to descend into chaos.

"Hey!" Drayton clapped his hands. "Hey."

The noise level dropped a notch then tapered off as all inhuman eyes turned on us as one. It was like looking into a shoal of piranha.

"This is a private meeting," Juno snapped. "Get out."

"We know," Drayton said. "And we're sorry for intruding. But we want to help."

Finlay's lip curled. "Really? Then you can tell the ocean hunters to give back my riders."

Juno rounded on him. "Fuck you, Finlay. I have already told you I do not have your men. Maybe this is all you. You took Leo and asked Killion to lay low to make it look like you are a victim too."

Finlay pointed at the necklace on her wrist. "You have my brother's fucking chain. He never takes that off."

Juno rolled her eyes and flicked her blonde tresses over her shoulder. "I told you, I found it. If I *had* taken him, I would not be so stupid as to parade his shit in your face, would I?"

Finlay snapped his mouth closed and pinched the bridge of his nose. "You're right. Damn it. We shouldn't be fighting amongst ourselves, we should be pooling our efforts and searching for our missing people."

Finally, some sense.

Juno nodded, and then, once again, all eyes were on us.

"Why are you here? Really?" Finlay asked.

Recalling Drayton's earlier words about not demanding answers and respect and all that, I licked my lips. "We'd *really* like to help."

Juno snorted and turned her head away. "This is kelpie business, and we take care of our own shit."

Finlay didn't contradict her, but then he didn't back her up either.

"I understand that, I do, but you're also a neph. You're one of us, and if someone is taking nephs, then we want to help get them back."

"More eyes, more hands," Finlay said. "Plus, they can scour inland, something we can't do effectively."

Juno tilted her chin to look up at the ceiling. "They could be somewhere inland. Yes." Her lips peeled back from her gums. "Held hostage, away from the sea, in pain. Wait. If they were hostages, surely we'd have received some kind of demands?" Her body went still as she made the neural connections. "No demands means whoever took them does not intend to return them. It means they could be dead."

"No," Finlay said. "If Killion was dead, I would know." He thumped his chest. "I would know here."

Juno nodded, suddenly less monster and more adrift female eager for a life raft. Her voice descended into a menacing growl. "I want Leo found, and I want the bastard who took him to pay."

That was all very well, but if we were going to find the missing kelpie we needed to figure out a motive for them being taken. "Is there anyone who has a grudge against either harras? Or someone who'd like to cause a fight between the ocean hunters and the sea riders?"

Finlay and Juno exchanged glances and then shook their heads.

This was going to be harder than expected. Okay, so I technically still had a case sitting in the car in a brown file, but maybe if I worked this one, it would warm me up for the cold case.

I ran a hand over my forehead. "Right, so we make a list of any connections between the missing kelpies — where they went and who they spoke to on the days leading up to their disappearance. We look for patterns, any aspects in common. Drayton and I can then check out any inland leads, and you guys can deal with the coast. Agreed?"

Once again, Finlay and Juno exchanged glances and nodded. Now that we had a direction, a working method, the atmosphere had calmed considerably.

"And the ripper activity?" Juno asked. "We cannot ignore that."

"It could be related, but it's most likely a coincidence," Drayton said. "The scourge has been acting strange lately. Things are changing, and it's something the Protectorate is looking into."

He was referring to Arachne's revelation that cracks had formed in the magic surrounding Arcadia and her assertion that something was coming.

Juno pouted in thought. "Very well. We will discuss and have the information ready for tomorrow."

Finlay inclined his head. "We accept your offer of aid."

But you can piss off now, was the

unspoken second half of that sentence. "We'll leave you to it then."

Drayton held the door open for me, and I escaped back into the lively, carefree air of the club.

Drayton let out a low whistle. "Looks like we have two cases to go over now."

And I wasn't going to neglect my cold case. "Hey, the cold case is MED, so their medical examiner would have dealt with the body, right?"

"Right." Drayton's eyes lit up. "You think we need to start from scratch and examine all the evidence with a trained neph eye?"

I grinned. "Yep. I think we need to go see Tristan."

"Good call on the cold case, by the way," Drayton said. "You're a natural at this investigative stuff. Ryker usually does that side of things when we partner up."

"Let me guess, you're the negotiator?"

He chuckled. "Something like that. And if that fails, we both kick some ass."

The road whizzed by, a lonely stretch that linked onto the main road that would lead us to the heart of the district. The street lights were few and far between, but that didn't seem to bother Drayton. He probably had preternatural vision anyway.

This was nice. This was good. Working with Drayton felt right. Being held by him felt right. No. Don't think about that. Think about the case, the job, and the next steps. Damn, how was I going to see him every day, be near him every day, and not ache for him? Stupid question. I'd probably be doing a lot of aching, simply to no avail.

He cleared his throat and flicked a glance my way. "Look, about earlier, on the dance floor, I—"

Something darted out into the road. Drayton yanked on the wheel, swerving to try and avoid hitting the creature, but something smashed into the windscreen. A pop and hiss filled the air, and then the car went into a tailspin. The world seemed to spin forever before careening to a screeching halt. The smell of burned rubber was sharp and hot in my nostrils.

"Serenity? Are you all right?"

I pressed a hand to my forehead. "Yeah. Just really bad déjà vu."

He unbuckled his seat belt. "I think we hit something. I need to check."

My skin prickled with foreboding, sudden and unexpected. "Wait." I gripped his arm. "Don't."

"What?"

It was impossible to see outside through the cracked windscreen. There was very little light, and smoke was billowing up around us. Where was the smoke coming from? Wait. There'd been several loud pops. Punctures.

"The tires are punctured." I stared at him wide-eyed. "This was deliberate."

His brow cleared in realization, and he reached into the back seat for his sword. My phone began to buzz, Cassie's name flashing urgently on caller ID.

"Cassie?"

"Harker. Thank fuck you're okay. Look, get back here now. I have a bad feeling. I need you both back here now."

My hands began to burn.

"Serenity, watch out."

My passenger side window exploded inwards.

"Harker!" Cassie's voice was a screech on the other end of the line.

Drayton tugged me toward him. His eyes fixed on our attacker. His face contorted with a mixture of wrath and horror, and then the air grew thick, stinging my nostrils and my throat. It was a familiar feeling, an awful feeling. Drayton's arms slipped from around me, and then the world fell into darkness.

"Serenity, wake up."

My head felt fuzzy and throbbed dully, and my lids were super heavy. I pulled them open to find Drayton's face staring at me from between bars.

Bars!

I sat up so fast my head spun. "What happened?"

A cage, we were in a cage. Separate cages. We were bathed in a weird green glow, but the room around us was shrouded in darkness. Fucking hell with the aversion to light in this damned district.

Drayton reached for my hand through the bars of his cell. "Listen to me carefully. We don't have much time." His throat bobbed. "The Breed have us. They want to hurt me." He was breathing hard. "Things will happen. Things I can't control." His voice cracked. "I don't want to hurt you. Please, do whatever you need to in order to protect yourself." He grabbed my wrist. "Whatever it takes, Serenity."

What did he mean? The Breed ... Wait, this was something to do with why he hated them. They wanted to hurt him. We needed to get out of here. My daggers.

"I can cut through the bars. I just need to make the daggers appear."

His eyes lit up. "You can do that?"

"The voice said I could." Although I hadn't wanted to believe it. "He said I need to assimilate with the darkness."

"Do you know how?"

I grabbed the bars between us to quell the quiver in my stomach. "No. But I can try."

Drayton's fingers curled around mine. "Do it."

I nodded and dropped my shields all the way. Ambrosius had said that the darkness was my subconscious and that it controlled the daggers. If connected with it, I'd be in control of the blades. It surged up to meet me now. The hunger burned steadily. It flooded my limbs as if searching for something. Come on, where were the daggers? I'd let the darkness out, relinquished the leash, what now? The darkness crawled up to caress the back of my neck and trickle over my scalp, testing and teasing. My pulse raced as panic gripped me. The darkness ran its fingers over my brain, preparing...

Preparing for what? Panic was a vise around my heart, squeezing painfully so it was impossible to draw breath.

"Serenity, it's okay. You're okay?"

My eyes burned, and I slammed my fists against the bars. "I want to do this. I can do this."

But my body had other ideas, rebelling at the thought of the invasion.

Drayton slipped a hand through the bars and cupped my cheek. "Look at me, Serenity Harker. You are the most amazing woman I have ever had the pleasure to know. Your strength of character, your convictions, and your morality never cease to stun me. You've spent your whole life protecting yourself from your demon, and assimilating won't be so easy. This, whatever happens here, is not your responsibility and it's not your fault. Remember that."

"What?"

His hand slid to the back of my neck. He tugged me forward and leaned in to press his lips to mine through the gap in the metal. It was a soft, tender kiss, a kiss filled with possibilities of what could have been. Hot tears stung my eyes and the back of my nose, and fear unfurled in my chest.

I pulled back. "Drayton? What do they want? What—"

"Well, well. Isn't this the touching scene."

Drayton's fingers slid from my cheek, his eyes shadowing with sorrow. He sat back, and his mask slipped back into place—the lazy, cocky mask that I'd seen when we'd first met.

"Hello, Max," Drayton drawled. "Any chance of an upgrade in accommodations?"

A man stepped out of the shadows—tall, lithe, and dressed in a black turtleneck sweater. It was the man from The Deep.

His smile was humorless. "Hello, Drayton. You know why you're here, don't you?"

Drayton shrugged a shoulder. "You missed me?"

Max's eyes narrowed. "Drop the act, incubus. I can smell your fear."

Drayton winced. "Nope, that's probably just my new cologne. I'll need to change it once I get out of here."

Max's lips parted in a toothy smile. "Yes. Once *you* get out." He turned his attention to me. "But you won't be going anywhere."

My heart thudded hard against my ribs. "What do you want from us?"

Max cocked his head. "You don't know." He waved a finger between Drayton and me. "He didn't tell you?"

"Max..." Drayton's tone was saturated with warning.

Max ignored him. "Drayton and I go way back, several years actually. We have a bond. You see, he killed my mate."

Drayton sat forward. "Your mate was a killer."

Max shrugged. "Maybe. But he was mine. You took him away from me, and I made you a promise. I promised to make you pay."

Drayton's control snapped. "And you did. You fucking did."

"Yes. I thought I had. I thought I'd ripped out your heart and left you broken, but then I saw you with her. That look on your face, one you never had for your beloved human, Viola. It occurred to me then that I'd acted hastily in my grief. Viola was never in your heart."

"Viola meant the world to me."

"Yes. Yes, I believe that, and maybe you even loved her in a way, the way a master loves a pet. But this woman, this nephilim ... she is different. She has your heart, and tonight, I will crush it. I will—" He broke off and tilted his head as if listening to something, his gaze growing unfocused as he nodded. "You may call us savage for taking what we need. For satiating our carnal pleasures and hunger as we see fit. But that is the nature of the beast, of the predator. But the beauty of The Breed is the ability to be both beast and man, and I will do you this one small courtesy. Something you did not offer me. I will give you the chance to say goodbye."

He stepped back into the gloom, and a shadow shifted with him. A man-shaped shadow. What the fuck? I blinked and the apparition was gone. Damn, the stark contrast of light and dark was playing tricks on my vision.

Drayton sat still for a long beat, his chest rising and falling, and then he inhaled deeply and slowly exhaled.

"Drayton? What's going on?" I hated the tremble in my voice.

"The daggers come out when you're in danger, right? They protect you?"

I nodded. "Yes."

He turned his head to look at me, his dark eyes blazing with a strange inner fire. "Promise me you will use them. Promise me you will defend yourself."

"Of course I will. If he attacks me, I'll be able to get us out of here."

Drayton licked his lips. "It's not him you'll need to defend yourself against."

"Then who?"

"Me."

Ice trickled through my veins. No, not him. He meant the demon inside him.

He shuffled closer to the bars separating us. "Listen to me, Serenity. Shit is going to happen, and it won't be pretty." His voice choked up, and he cleared his throat. "When it's over, I'll be gone. It'll be the demon you'll be dealing with, and that fucker is heartless. He doesn't care about anything but feeding. There is no Bane for you to load up on sexual energy from. There is no bringing me back. No reasoning. Do you understand?"

My neck was tight and stiff with fear.

He gripped my face with both hands, pulling me toward the bars so we were almost nose to nose. "Serenity, the incubus *will* kill you. Do you understand? He will kill you, so you *must* kill him first."

No. Killing the incubus would mean killing Drayton. I couldn't hurt him. "There has to be another way." I squeezed my eyes shut and willed the darkness to take me. There was panic, but it was a cocktail of anxiety mingled with the fear of losing Drayton, of having to hurt him. Nothing happened. The darkness sat heavy at the back of my mind, silent for the first time in forever.

Ambrosius? Ambrosius, I need you.

But even the voice of my daggers was silent.

Anger was a helix swirling inside me. I opened my eyes, dislodging teardrops. Fuck this. I needed this to work. Why wasn't it working? I wanted to assimilate. I wanted it, and it was out of reach. Damn Ambrosius, damn him for not being here to guide me through this.

"Serenity. Please..." Drayton pressed his forehead to the bars. "I can't go through this again. I can't kill another person I love. I won't."

Love? He loved me. The rest of his words sank in. "Viola? You killed her?"

He looked up sharply. "Yes. I killed her. I fucked her until every drop of her life force was gone. I was powerless, and the incubus was in control, caring nothing for anyone or anything but my survival. But there was a moment when I caught a glimpse of her, when I managed to rise up out of the darkness, and I knew that she hadn't fought. She didn't fight the demon. But you need to fight, do you understand, because your sister needs you, and the humans at the House of Vitae need you. You *must* live."

I reached for him, and the echo of bootfalls filled the room. With a final lingering look, Drayton withdrew from me. He stood up, his body tense and ready for what they were going to do to him.

Four members of The Breed strode out of the shadows surrounding our prison. Huge guys with yellow eyes sporting vertical, narrow cat pupils. They studied Drayton in silence, and then they began to laugh. It was a high-pitched, horrifically mocking sound that chilled me to the bone.

"Come on then, you ugly fuckers," Drayton said. "Do your worst."

One of them unlocked Drayton's cage, and they all piled in. The next few minutes were filled with the sound of fists on flesh, of boots cracking ribs. Drayton fought, but he was outnumbered and out-massed. My screams and taunts for them to let me out, to try shit on me, were ignored—eclipsed by their crazy laughter. That ear-grating laughter muted Drayton's moans of pain, but it couldn't quell the spatter of blood and the crunch of bone. Finally, Drayton's cries stopped. They piled out of the cage, locked it, and vanished into the dark. Drayton lay in the fetal position with his back to me. Was he breathing? Please let him be breathing. His shoulders rose and fell, but the movement was erratic. How many broken ribs did he have? How long before his demon healed him?

"Drayton. Drayton. Oh, God." I pushed my arm through the gap, straining to reach him. It was no use. He was too far away. There was nothing to do but wait. Wait and try to assimilate with the darkness.

Ambrosius? Please...

Drayton moaned and rolled onto his back. His face was a mess. Cuts and bruises and swelling, but then he began to heal before my eyes. Slow at first, then faster and faster until his skin was smooth and unmarred.

He sat up fast. "Where? Where are they?"

"Gone. They're gone." A sob caught in my throat. "You're okay. You made it."

"No. Damn it." He ran a hand over his face. "They're not gone."

The four Breed males strode back into the circle of light, and the torture began again. Eyes screwed shut, I rocked, unable to watch, not wanting to hear, and suddenly their plan was clear. They were going to beat him and force him to expel power in order to heal the wounds, because that's what his demon would do. It would heal him to ensure his survival. They'd do it again and again until there was no power left, until Drayton was gone, leaving behind his demon, and then...

How long before his reserves were tapped out? How long before he was gone, and I was left alone with his incubus side?

My throat was clogged with tears, head pounding with impotent rage by the time they were done. Three rounds of kicking. The third time, he'd barely regained consciousness before they'd laid into him. And now he was still and silent as the dead.

"Drayton? Drayton, can you hear me?"

The transformation this time was different. His wounds knit, his bruises healed, but his skin took on an ashy color, his cheeks grew gaunter, and his lips thinned. I backed away from the bars separating us. Drayton was gone.

"Do you love him?"

I started in surprise to find Max outside my cage. He'd moved so stealthily, I hadn't heard a sound.

"Do you?" he pressed.

Did I? I cared about him and I wanted him, yearned for him, but... "I don't know. It's too soon to tell. I barely know him. I..." My voice cracked. "Please don't do this."

Something akin to empathy flashed across his face, but he schooled his features too fast for me to latch on to his momentary lapse.

"I loved my mate. I loved him with every little piece of my soul, and when he died, he took a part of me with him. I want Drayton to know what that feels like. I want him broken. I believed he loved Viola, but it seemed she died for nothing."

"He did love her."

"No. That wasn't love. Love means you go to the ends of the earth to be with someone. Love means finding a way to be together no matter what."

"What are you talking about?"

"Do you think if my mate was a mere mile or so away in a cemetery I would let anything hold me back from seeing him, being with him, spending time with him? No. But Drayton did not go to see Viola. He stayed away. His guilt is greater than his love for her. Guilt because he knows he did not love her. Not in the way she deserved. But you... I saw it in his eyes tonight at The Deep—the torment and the pain. His heart is in thrall. Killing you will break him, and I shall finally have my revenge."

Drayton stirred.

"Well, it was nice talking with you. I'll be back later to clean up the mess." He offered me a mock salute and strode off into the shadows.

The bars between Drayton and me rose out

of the way with a whirr, and Drayton opened his eyes.

Drayton sat up slowly and then turned his head to look at me. His eyes were so dark they were almost black, and when he smiled it was a cruel, mocking action.

"Hello, Serenity," he said. "We meet again." He glanced about, taking in the bars. "And it seems that this time there is no escape."

I held up my hands. "You don't want to hurt me. Drayton wouldn't want that."

He stood fluidly but didn't make a move toward me. "What Drayton wants could kill him. It's my job to protect him."

"By killing me?"

"Exactly."

My hands began to burn, and the heat of adrenaline flooded me. Drayton was gone. This was the incubus, and he wanted me dead.

The incubus licked his lips. "If I kill you, all these dangerous feelings Drayton has will go away. You may have tricked me once. Down in the dungeons of the Protectorate, you succeeded in putting Drayton back in control with your little ploy. But it's different this time. He's buried too deep. This time, I *will* end you, and I *will* save him."

The incubus lunged, and I dove out of the way, onto his side of the cage. He smashed against the bars, spun back around, and headed straight for me. Drayton was a big guy, solid muscle, and the incubus was single-minded determination in the body of a mini tank. How long could I evade before he got his hands on me?

"Stop running and accept your fate. I promise I'll make it quick." He swayed from side to side. "I'm so hungry." He leapt, and this time I wasn't fast enough.

His body smashed into mine, propelling me to the ground. His hands fisted in my hair, legs tangling with mine to hold me immobile. My hands were on fire as if torn with the decision of releasing the blades or holding fire. Ambrosius was right, the darkness was me, the demon was me, and it was holding back because it sensed my conflict—because there had to be another way.

"Please. Drayton, don't do this. Please."

The incubus wearing Drayton's face leaned in and licked my face, his tongue warm and wet against my cheek. A shudder ran through me, part desire and part dread.

"You want this." He ground into my thigh. "You want me." He crushed his mouth to mine, forcing his tongue past my lips, and began to feed.

The blades materialized in my hands, heavy and solid. Tears burned my eyes and leaked down the sides of my face. He was taking and taking and there was no choice.

I stabbed him in the back.

He tore his lips away to bellow in pain before scrambling off me. His gaze fell to the daggers in my hand and there was genuine surprise there. He hadn't known. How could he have not known?

Move, Serenity.

Ambrosius.

Hope fluttered in my chest. I rolled to my feet and ran for the door. If I could slice open the lock with my daggers...

No, you need to finish him. If you don't, he will hunt you. There will be no escape.

I can't. I won't.

My blade slid through metal and the lock came away, but before I could push it through and open the doors, Drayton's arm slipped around my throat. He pulled me tight against him and pressed me into the bars at the same time. I was stuck, held immobile with my right arm trapped at a strange angle, the dagger hanging uselessly from my fingers. My left hand was free but trapped between the bars.

"Drop the daggers," he said.

"I can't." My voice was a choked rasp.

"Drop them!"

"I literally can't. They're stuck to my hands."

He spun me around and head-butted me. The world exploded into starlight and pain and then my wrists were held captive and his mouth was latched onto mine again. He began to feed. My energy rose up from my solar plexus, into my throat, and poured into his mouth.

No, Serenity. You need to fight. You need to fight or you will die. Ambrosius's voice was clear in my head, and close on its heels was the echo of Drayton's words. *...you need to fight, do you understand? Because your sister needs you and the humans at the House of Vitae need you. You must live...*

Live. I had to live. I *wanted* to live.

Power was rushing out of me, into Drayton, into the incubus, but I wasn't done yet. I had a reserve, I always kept a reserve, and this time it was Bane's power—potent and strong. Yes. Bane was strong. All I needed to do was channel that strength. As if summoned by my conviction, Bane's energy poured through me and seeped into my muscles. It was the boost I needed to twist my wrists out of Drayton's grasp, and the insanity I needed to bring up my daggers and sink them into his ribs. The blades cut through his flesh and bone like it was melted butter.

"I'm sorry. So sorry."

His mouth slid from mine with a sharp intake of breath, and he raised his head to look at me in utter horror. The darkness bled out of his eyes, leaving me staring into warm brown ones. Blood bubbled from between his lips, and he toppled backwards.

I reached for him, falling to the floor in a crouch with him half in my arms. Drayton was back. He'd overcome his demon, but I'd killed him. My daggers had killed him.

Serenity, we have to go. We have to go now. Before whoever brought you here comes back. I can help you. I can guide you.

But I couldn't tear my eyes from Drayton, couldn't peel my hands from his face, his hair, and couldn't stop the sobs that wracked my chest.

His eyes rolled in his head, finally coming to rest on me.

"Yes." I stroked his cheek. "I'm here. Stay with me. Come on. Get up." I strained to rise with him clutched against me.

He grabbed the front of my shirt. "No. Dying. Serenity…" My name was a wet gurgle. "You need … to run." He released me, shoving me away with the last of his strength. "Run now."

His eyes fluttered closed as he exhaled

slow and long.

"Drayton? Dray?"

He's gone, and if you do not move, then his death will have been in vain. So move.

Dead. He was dead, and I'd killed him. I had to get out. I had to stay alive. For him. For Drayton.

I lowered him gently to the ground. I couldn't leave him here, but I couldn't carry him with me. Oh, God.

Serenity Harker. Get yourself out of here, now. You must not be captured. You must not die.

I turned to the cage door and the lock I'd cut out with my blades—the blades that had now deserted me. Thank God I'd cut it because otherwise I'd have been stuck. Taking a step back, I delivered a hard kick to the door. The lock fell to the ground with a chink and the door grated open.

I was free.

Not yet. Not until we're above ground. Now move.

The cage room wasn't even a room. It was a chamber in a network of chambers. We were underground again. The walls glowed with an eerie green light emanating from some kind of luminescent algae. This was another burrow like Arachne's. Who knew, maybe it was the same burrow. Which way was out? How long before they found me?

Take a left here. Yes. Stop, allow your senses to taste the air. Can you feel it? Can you feel the breeze?

No. I just … Drayton was dead.

Keep moving. Just keep moving.

We came to an intersection, and a strange awareness skittered across my scalp.

Take a right here.

My feet faltered.

Serenity, take the right.

There's something this way. I took several steps down the left tunnel.

We do not have time for this. We need to move now.

But the senses he'd just been talking about had kicked into gear, carrying me farther down into the left tunnel and into a chamber similar to the one Drayton and I had… My throat tightened and pinched. Don't think about him now. I moved toward the glow, toward the cages.

Two figures sat inside, leaning up against the bars. Both looked up as I approached. The one closest to me scrambled to his feet and rushed forward.

"You," he said. "How did you get in here? Are you with *them*?"

The two missing kelpies. What the heck were they doing here? "Killion?" I looked to the other guy. "And Leo. Your friends are looking for you. Where are the others?"

"Dead," Killion said. His eyes narrowed. "You're not with them. Good. There are keys on the far wall on a hook. Get us out."

There was indeed a hook on the wall with a bunch of keys hanging from it. There was also a long table loaded with strange equipment made for slicing and hurting.

"Quick, before they return," Killion urged.

I found the correct keys for the locks in two tries, and the kelpies staggered out of their prison.

"Follow me."

"You know a way out?" Leo asked.

"I think so."

It was all about silence and stealth and speed. I'd been lucky so far. The tunnels had been empty, but luck had a way of running out.

"How are you here?" Killion hissed.

"They kidnapped me and Drayton. I got away."

"And Drayton?"

"Dead."

There would be time to trade stories later, time to dwell and grieve. Time to figure out what the fuck The Breed were up to and why they'd wanted two kelpies. There would be time to plot revenge. The kelpies moved slow, their gaits more a stagger than a lope. They needed the sea, no doubt. They'd already been away from it much too long.

Leo stopped to brace himself against the

wall and Killion paused to check on him.

We must keep moving. Can you not sense the disturbance in the air? They are coming. They know you have escaped.

I gripped Killion's arm. "The Breed know we're free. They're looking for us."

Killion nodded curtly. "Leo, we need to keep going. Can you make it?"

Leo clenched his teeth and nodded.

Just another few minutes and we'd be out, I could sense it now, the fresh air with a strange briny tang,

Killion and Leo sped up, as if sensing it too.

The sea. It was the sea.

An intersection loomed and voices echoed through the tunnels behind us. "This way. They came this way," they said.

Shit. They'd found us.

I began to jog, and then something grabbed the back of my shirt, halting my progress.

I flailed. "What?"

Killion dragged me toward him. "We are in your debt for saving our lives, and if you survive, we will pay. But for now, we need a diversion."

He gripped my arm, and then a crack resounded through the tunnel. For a moment, I wondered at the sound, at what could make such an awful noise of finality, and then the pain hit—slugging me in the chest and squeezing my lungs in an iron grip. My scream was an involuntary shriek. Killion shoved me away, and I slid to the ground, burning with agony, unable to think, to move. Their bootfalls were a receding echo as they made their escape.

Get up. Serenity, get up. The enemy approaches. Get up and you can still be free. Get up or Drayton will have died for nothing. You killed him. You'd have killed him for nothing.

Drayton's face flashed before my eyes; his words echoed in my ear. He'd wanted me to live. He'd made me promise. The Breed was close — their whoops and howls filtered toward me. If they caught me... There was no waiting to find out. Cradling my broken arm, I pulled myself to my feet and ran. Every step, every beat of my soles on the ground was a jarring movement that sent fire through my arm, but stopping meant more pain. Stopping meant death. Through the tunnels, rising upward with The Breed at my back, I ran. The air grew cold, and then a breeze bathed me in a welcome chill as I slid up a chute. My aching sobs were a symphony to my determination as I pushed at the earth and the sand to slide free onto rock.

They were behind me.

Using my knees and the toes of my boots for purchase, I propelled myself out.

Cover it, pack in the dirt. Do it now.

Holding my broken arm close to my chest, I kicked the dirt back into place, rocks and sand

and more rocks. Finally, it was done. I had to go, get back to the mansion. The others needed to know what had happened, they needed to know...

Where was I? How far from home was this place? Leaving the chute behind, feet slipping and sliding in a stumble over the stony terrain, I rounded a large, dark rock. The sea air slapped me in the face, and my questions were answered.

Midnight stared back at me from across an expanse of water. The lights of The Deep lay far to my left. The rocky ground underfoot made sense now. I'd seen this place from the shore. I was trapped on Desert Rock.

"The Breed will come. They'll find me. There is nowhere to run and I can't swim, not like this."

My body had gone numb, the pain a dull thing in the background of the adrenaline coursing through my veins.

Ambrosius was silent.

"Ambrosius? Are you there?"

His absence was an empty cavern. I was alone. My resolve almost cracked, but once again Drayton was with me, in my mind, in my heart, urging me on. Whispering, *think, think, Harker*. How to get across. How to call for help.

Call for help?

The kelpies... Cassie had called them with rocks.

Rocks were aplenty here.

I picked one up and, biting back a scream of pain, flung it into the sea. I didn't wait to see if they came, but picked up another, and another, flinging them as fast as I could. They'd come. One of the kelpies would come.

They had to.

And then a head broke the surface of the water about three or four meters out.

"Help! Help me, please."

The head began to move toward the island, and my heart lifted with hope. A shadow fell over me, blocking out the moon for a moment before releasing it from its clutches. What was it? A bird? I raised my chin to scan the night sky, which stared back at me, twinkling with innocent stars.

"Hello, little neph."

A fist of fear clamped itself to the nape of my neck. I knew that arrogant tone. I turned slowly to face the Black Wing.

Abigor smiled, and then his gaze fell to my arm, held close to my chest, and his brows snapped down. "What happened to you?"

Would he help me? If he knew what The Breed were doing, would he do something to stop them? Maybe he'd get Drayton out.

"There's a chute back there." I jerked my head. "I was underground. The Breed had me and Drayton ... Drayton is still down there. They kidnapped us."

He considered this for a moment and then shrugged. "Maximilian has a severe dislike for Drayton. You're lucky you escaped."

"That's it? That's all you have to say? Aren't you going to stop them? You're a fucking Black Wing. Do something."

His eyes were suddenly alight with an inner fire and his lips turned down. "There is nothing to do, because everything, *everything*, is pointless. Everything except the daggers etched into your pretty skin."

"Just leave me alone." I took a step away from him.

"There is nowhere to run, neph. Despite Bane's assurances to keep you safe, I find you in trouble yet again. I believe that forfeits his deal with Abbadon. At least I'm sure I can convince Abbadon of that."

Where was the kelpie I'd summoned with the pebble? Had it landed yet? "Have you been stalking me?"

"No. For if I had, you would not have been in trouble. I simply keep my ear to the ground, and I heard about the accident. I heard you were missing, so I took a short flight." He cocked his head. "Now it's time for us to take a flight together."

"Look, I just want to go back to the mansion. If you can take me there, back to Bane, then I'm sure he'll be very grateful."

"Grateful? Bane?" Abigor snorted. "I'm

more likely to see a sunrise in Midnight."

He began to amble toward me slowly, at his leisure, because, heck, he had all the time in the world. Even if that kelpie had landed, it was unlikely to go up against a Black Wing.

Abigor was going to take me. There was no getting away from that.

"Are you going to hold me prisoner in your clifftop mansion?"

He smiled. "You'll be very comfortable there."

"If you take me, then it's against my will. I want to go back to Bane. Back to the Protectorate, where I belong. If you take me by force, they'll search for me, they'll find me."

"They will search, no doubt. But no one comes to the mansion without an invitation. No one would dare."

Please, let the kelpie have heard this. Please …

He held out his arms. "Now, do you wish to remain here in the cold, with a broken limb, or will you come with me? I can take you by force, but I imagine with that arm at such an angle, it could prove painful."

There was no choice, no other way off the island.

I stepped into his arms.

Abigor held me tight, but at an angle so as not to cause me too much pain. I buried my head in his chest and bit back tears of frustration. Drayton's body was in The Breed's possession. What would they do to him? I needed to get back and tell the others. We needed to mount a search and retrieve him and strike back at The Breed for what they'd done. Had Killion and Leo made it out successfully? Would they tell someone about Drayton? Probably not; they'd broken my arm and left me to die, not exactly something to confess to. If I'd left them to their fate, I'd have been able to swim to shore and maybe avoided Abigor. If I could go back and do things differently... I sighed. I'd still have helped them because that's who I was.

Damned Abigor and his obsession with the daggers. We landed lightly and Abigor released me. I stumbled back and sucked in a breath between my teeth as fresh pain lanced up my arm. My head throbbed and exhaustion tugged at my mind. We were on a balcony overlooking the tumultuous ocean.

"This will be your room," Abigor said.

Like hell I was staying here. "Where is Abbadon?"

Abigor smiled smugly. "Not here. And he won't be for several days." He canted his head. "You think you can influence him? Convince him to take you back to the Protectorate?"

I shrugged, then hissed as fire raced up my arm.

His face darkened. "You are in much pain."

"Well, a broken arm can do that." I didn't hold back on the sarcasm.

He nodded and then strode off the balcony. I trailed after him, into the room he'd allocated to me, but he was already gone. A quick inspection of the two doors showed one to be the ensuite bathroom and the other the locked exit. It was an unremarkable space. A small double bed, dresser, and wardrobe. There were no flourishes or extraordinary decorative features, but the carpet beneath my feet was soft and thick.

I perched on the edge of the bed. It was only a matter of time before someone came for me. Even if Killion and Leo kept their mouths shut about my fate, surely the kelpie, who I'd summoned, would say something? He or she must have heard my conversation with Abigor. Someone would come for me. They had to.

My chest throbbed, and my arm burned. It was getting harder to focus as the pain took over.

The door to the room opened, and a Black Wing I'd never seen walked in. He was slightly shorter than Abigor, lithe rather than built, and his face was etched in concern.

He stopped a meter away from me. "I sense a clean break. I can heal you. Would you allow me to heal you?"

"Who are you?"

"My name is Malphas." His smile was warm and genuine. "Will you permit me to heal you?"

Pride had no place here. I nodded. "Please."

He approached and crouched by me. "This may sting a little, but please remain still."

He raised his hands to hover over my broken arm. They began to glow with a soft, buttery light, and then my arm was on fire. A scream lodged in my throat, and then darkness claimed me.

Consciousness stole over me like the comfort of a blanket, and I made out the voices of Abigor and Malphas. I was half tempted to feign sleep for longer, but what if they simply locked the door and left? How could I convince them to let me go if they weren't even in the room?

"Is she all right?" Abigor asked.

"She will be," Malphas said.

I opened my eyes. "I'm fine." The pain was gone and my arm was whole again. I sat up on the bed. "I thought you said it would hurt a bit. That was ... something else."

Malphas winced. "Black Wings have a high pain threshold. To us, that would have been a slight stinging sensation."

Wow. "Well, it sucked, but thank you." I flexed my arm and made a fist with my hand. "It feels as good as new."

"You're welcome." Malphas gave me another warm smile, and my tense muscles relaxed.

"Did Abigor tell you I'm here against my will?"

Malphas looked to Abigor in confusion. "What does she mean?"

Abigor grimaced. "We do what we must to keep the daggers safe."

Malphas rubbed his temples as if fending off a headache. "This goes against everything we stand for. How *could* you?"

Abigor clenched his teeth. "Would you rather I'd left her to die? To be taken by The Breed again? Or dragged to the bottom of the ocean by the kelpies?"

No way. He was not making it out as if

he'd rescued me. "The kelpies were coming to help me. I summoned them."

"Oh, they would have helped you, all right. They would have helped you to kiss the seabed."

"Bullshit. I'm Protectorate. They wouldn't have harmed me, especially not when I told them that two of their own had been held by The Breed too."

Abigor's brows shot up. "The Breed was holding kelpies?"

"Yes."

Malphas and Abigor exchanged glances. "What in the world would they want with the sea dwellers?"

I crossed my arms under my breasts. "Take me back to the Protectorate now."

Malphas opened his mouth to respond, but Abigor cut him off.

"No. You belong here. We can keep you safe."

But I *needed* to go back, needed to be with the others and tell them about Drayton. I needed to cry, grieve, something, because breaking down here was not an option, not amongst these strangers who didn't give a damn about what I'd lost. To stem the tears, I summoned rage until it was hot lava boiling in my stomach.

I stood, hands fisted at my sides. "Take me back, or I swear to you, I will make you pay. I will find a way, and I will hurt you."

Abigor laughed.

"Abi, come on. This isn't how we operate. We cannot keep her prisoner. It is wrong. Abbadon—"

"Is a fool!" Abigor snapped. "His tolerant approach is what got us into this mess in the first place. He made the deal with the White Wings. He trapped us all here, and now we wait to fail."

What was he talking about?

Malphas shot me a panicked glance. "Abi, please."

Abigor ignored him and focused on me. "You want to know the truth, little neph? Well, here it is. This whole place—the city of Arcadia—is a fucking prison. A grand test for humanity, and guess what? They're failing, and the only thing we have that the White Wings don't are those daggers. It was Abbadon's idea to hand our only advantage to the Protectorate. And then those daggers chose you, and ever since they did, you've been getting into trouble, scrapes that could result in your demise and lead to the loss of the daggers. I am not letting them out of my sight again, which means *you* stay. Here." He spun on his heel and exited the room, slamming the door behind him.

"What is he talking about?"

Malphas sighed. "I suppose there is no harm in making you aware. There are only a handful of residents of Arcadia that know the truth. Bane is one of them."

"That it's a prison? So there *is* an outside world?"

"Oh, yes, Serenity. There's a big wide world with many oceans and cities, deserts and forests. It is a most beautiful, wondrous thing."

Hadn't Arcahne intimated the same when she'd said she'd come from outside? That she'd travelled into Arcadia through a breach? She'd said there were more creatures being drawn here, but for some reason the concept of a big wide world just hadn't sunk in, not until now.

He indicated the bed. "Sit and I will tell you." I perched on the edge of the mattress, and he pulled up a chair. "A long time ago, not long after the dawn of man, God left. We don't know where he went or why, he was just gone, leaving the winged to watch over his creation. To watch over man. Over time, two factions grew. One that believed that man didn't deserve to retain its free will, and another that worked to preserve it at all costs, claiming that it had been God's intention to gift man free will."

"The White Wings, they wanted to take free will…"

"Yes. And the Black Wings, we wanted to preserve it. Although back then we all had White Wings, it was only when the larger faction cast us out of heaven that our wings turned black. Once we lost the connection to the divine plane, we were cursed to never return. But we fought from here on earth. Hiding in plain sight and encouraging man to make his own choices. We fought the White Wings, and they knew that as long as we were alive, they would never win. So, they sought to kill us."

"Wait, I thought winged couldn't be killed?"

"You thought right. Only God can unmake one of the winged. But God was gone. However, he left behind a drop of his grace, just a tiny amount, and the White Wings used it to create five weapons — weapons that could kill a Black Wing. They gave these weapons to a mortal man who they blessed with strength, agility, and power."

Five weapons. "Are you talking about King Arthur? No, he's just a legend … a myth."

"Oh, he was very real. Although the tales of his round table and his knights have been twisted into something entirely different. In truth, Arthur was a violent, bloodthirsty warrior who hunted Black Wings on the instruction of the White Wings. And he killed many of us, so many, in fact, that our numbers began to dwindle. In the end, we had no choice but to strike back."

"You killed him?"

"No." Malphas shook his head. "We would never take a mortal life."

"So, what did you do?"

"We went to his confidant, his friend, and his ally, Merlin. We told him the truth. We told him what was at stake. Now, Merlin was no mortal, he was a man born of the union of Black Wing and human, one of the nephilim. Our blood coursed in his veins, and once we opened his eyes, he was able to finally understand his prophetic dreams."

"Wait, are you saying it was Merlin who killed Arthur?"

He nodded slowly. "Merlin took the weapons. He ran and hid. And he has been hiding ever since." He reached for my hands and turned them over to expose my wrists. "These daggers are the only thing he left behind — enchanted to remain in stone, resistant to all who tried to prize them out. Until you..."

I stared at the tattoos on my arms.

"We found them before the winged could. As far as we know, they aren't even aware of their existence. It is our only advantage against them, because, you see, we believe the daggers are a clue to Merlin's whereabouts. To the whereabouts of the weapons, and we must never let the White Wings get their hands on them, because if they do, the killing will begin again, and if the Black Wings are wiped out, there will be nothing standing in the way of the White Wings and humanity's free will. They will take it. They will take it all."

My heart was pounding so hard I was sure he could hear it. "And Arcadia? Why are we here?"

"After Merlin absconded with the weapons, the winged factions were at a stalemate. Our Morningstar, our leader, Lucifer, petitioned for a meeting with the powers."

"Powers?"

"Heaven has a hierarchy of its own—three spheres, to be precise. Angels were separated according to their principal function. The powers are part of the second sphere—warrior angels responsible for making sure that the cosmos stay in order. Lucifer was once a power, and so he sought to speak to his brothers, but they refused to meet with him. And then ... Lucifer disappeared."

"What do you mean he disappeared?"

Malphas's face was a map of sorrow. "He was gone. Just like God before him. We searched far and wide, but there was no sign of him."

"And the meeting with the powers?"

"Was finally granted. Abbadon went in Lucifer's place. And from that meeting, Arcadia was born. A place where we would remain for a century. A place where humanity would be tested with the horrors of the world. The magic, which warps, is a metaphor for the ills of the outside world, and humanity's endurance and faith are tested. Arcadia is a place where we can test to see if free will is in humanity's best interests, or if they would give it up for sanctuary. The only proviso was no interference by either side. No Black Wing or White Wing could coerce humans, save humans, or hurt humans."

It was beginning to make sense now. "So, you employed the nephilim to protect them on our behalf?"

Malphas's green eyes twinkled. "Yes. At first, when we lay with humans, it was for comfort, but after Arthur began killing us, Lucifer ordered us to procreate, to make nephilim, because he knew that one day, our numbers would need to be swelled."

Arcadia was a testing ground. This whole city was a lie. "How do we get out?"

"A century was the limit, and we are almost upon that, but the White Wings are winning. Despite the nephilim's efforts to keep humans safe, too many humans have given up their free will. Every twenty-five years, if the Black Wings were winning, outsiders would come to balance out the human population. But the last twenty-five-year mark came and went with no new entrants."

"How much time do we have left?"

"A year, maybe less."

"Then what?"

"Then the White Wings will take the world, and we will be honor-bound by oath to sit back and allow them to do it."

No. That couldn't happen. "We need to stop them. We need to tell the humans."

His expression hardened. "You cannot. Do

you understand? For if you do, the contract will be void, and the White Wings will win by default."

"What's stopped *them* from telling the humans and just taking the win?"

"They have taken an oath not to do so; it ties their tongues and they cannot physically speak the words."

"But you can?"

"Yes. Cruel temptation, for can you imagine how often the words have hovered on our tongues? It is a relief speaking them to you. The only stipulation in the contract is that a Black Wing or nephilim cannot reveal the truth to a human."

"So, what *can* we do?"

He glanced at my wrists again. "The Black Wings can't do anything, but the nephilim can. They can keep on fighting. They can keep humanity safe."

And the Black Wings needed to keep me out of the White Wings' clutches. I was more than a prisoner. I was the possible key to a set of deadly weapons. My heart sank. "Abbadon won't let me leave, will he?"

Malphas tucked in his chin. "Your life is important. We have no idea what your demise could mean for the daggers, and although Abigor's methods are harsh, his logic is not flawed."

"What about The Order. Have you

considered speaking to them? They could know what the daggers are for. Maybe they can even remove them from my skin."

His face tightened. "The Order is misguided. You must stay away from them at all costs."

"But—"

"Rest, and I will bring you some food. Tomorrow, I will show you around your new home."

My new home? No. It couldn't be. I wouldn't let it. If they weren't going to let me go, then I'd have to find a way to escape.

I dreamed of Drayton, of his hands cupping my face and his breath warm on my lips. He was about to kiss me, and my heart was in my throat with anticipation, but before his lips could brush mine, he jerked back, his eyes wide with horror. Blood dribbled out of his mouth.

"You killed me. How could you kill me?" he said.

I awoke to tears on my face and an ache in my heart that was so deeply embedded I doubted it would ever recede. A knock sounded on my door and then Malphas appeared with a breakfast tray. I sat up, wiping at my tears, and his face contracted in empathy. He set the tray on the bedside table and fixed a huge smile on his face.

"Eat and dress, then we will explore the mansion together."

His kindness was a balm that took the edge

off my sorrow. He left me to it. Deep breath. Today was a new day. Today, I would make a mental map of this place, and then I'd make my escape.

The food was good: eggs, bacon, toast, and beans. When was the last time I'd eaten a cooked breakfast like this? Probably over a month ago. Jesse made the best weekend breakfasts. We'd lounge on the sofa reading afterwards. If I had to work, I'd make sure I had the afternoon shift so we could still have our mornings. God, how I missed her.

Malphas returned a half hour later. "Are you ready to see your new home?"

I nodded and smiled. Let him think I was on board, that I'd given up hope of leaving. He'd be much more inclined to let down his guard then.

I followed him out into a wide hallway decorated in soft magnolia colors. It was modern and cozy and nothing like the dark, forbidding place it pretended to be from the outside. The floors were carpeted in thick, dark pile, and fancy lighting was fixed to the walls.

"I didn't expect everything to look so new and modern."

"It didn't use to be," Malphas said. "But after we were here for several decades, Abbadon decided to begin renovations. It's taken a while, but we're finally comfortable."

We padded past large French windows

overlooking a sloping garden.

"It leads to a track that takes you down to the beach," Malphas provided. "Maybe in a few weeks, we can go? I can fly you over the walls."

A few weeks? Yes. They'd need to make sure I was settled and no longer wanting to make a run for it.

I nodded politely. "That would be nice."

We descended a short flight of stairs onto another floor. How high up were we? It was impossible to tell with the house being on a cliff. It threw my perspective completely off. This floor was much of the same: corridors, locked doors, and wide hallways.

Malphas stopped outside a dark wooden door. "This is the library. Do you like to read?"

"Yes. I do."

He smiled and opened the door before standing back to usher me through. Now this was a room to spend time in. It was huge, filled with books slotted neatly into cases that stretched up to a high ceiling. There was a wide grate, not lit, but probably impressive when filled with a roaring fire. I ran my fingers along the spines of the books nearest to me, titles I'd never heard of bound in leather with golden words pressed into the spines.

"Would you like to come here later?"

This time my smile was genuine. If I was going to be stuck here for some time, then reading was a good way to while away the hours. "I'd like that."

The rest of the tour was mundane in comparison, but my mental map was building. With each extra hallway or room I added, with each window or door I etched into my mind, came a sinking sensation because there was no way out. The grounds were bordered by high gates, locked at all times, because why would they need to use gates when they could fly in and out. But they kept out regular nephs and, in my case, would keep me in. The other side of the house was the ocean. Squashing the hopelessness, I continued to build my map. And then he led me to a set of French doors and into a wide courtyard filled with fighting Black Wings.

On closer inspection, they weren't fighting, they were sparring—some hand-to-hand and some with weapons—and overseeing it, his steely gaze fixed on the scene, was Abigor.

He turned to us with a frown. "What are you doing, Malphas? I thought we agreed we would keep her indoors for the first week."

"She can hardly escape from the courtyard," Malphas pointed out.

He was right. The damned space was at the center of the building. There was nowhere to run but back into the house. But escape was the last thing on my mind right now. It was impossible to tear my gaze away from the Black Wings, so many of them and so magnificent as they thrust and parried and leapt and rolled. Their powerful wings worked with them, raising up or tucking in tight to avoid the sharp edge of a blade.

"They're training." Abigor's tone was saturated with pride.

"Training for what?"

The corner of Abigor's mouth lifted. "War."

War? "What war?"

Malphas tutted. "Abi, please."

"She is blood of our blood, and she should know what we have in store, for she may very well fight alongside us."

This was intriguing. "What are you talking about?"

"We made a vow to protect humanity. We vowed to our creator that we would guard them, watch over them, and allow them free will, and we will not go back on our word, not for any contract or treaty, because our promise to our creator supersedes everything."

My pulse kicked up. They were planning to fight. If the White Wings won, they were planning war against them. I looked to Malphas but his attention was on Abigor, and the expression on his face was murderous.

Abigor glanced down his nose at me, scanning my face and reading my thoughts etched there, no doubt. "Yes, little neph, you have it. You have it."

Metal continued to clash against metal,

shields clashed against spears, and whips cracked on the ground. The army of Black Wings prepared for battle, and for some reason, my blood began to sing.

The fire had been lit in the library and the hearth roared in welcome as I stepped inside.

"I'll be back to check on you in an hour," Malphas said. "I will need to lock you in." He winced apologetically.

My stomach tightened, reminding me that no matter how nice he was being, he was still my guard, and this was my prison.

Averting my gaze, I nodded. "That's fine. I'll be fine."

He retreated, and the scrape of the key in the lock raised a flutter of panic. I exhaled. It was just a room, a beautiful room, not a cage. Not this time anyway. The seat by the fire beckoned, but I needed a book first. Something to pass the hour. The room was larger than it looked at first glance, and the shelves stretched back into the gloom lit only by weak amber light. The tomes here were older, the leather battered and worn. There was a whole shelf of black leather-bound books written in a language I didn't understand. One moment it was clear and the next it wasn't.

Latin.

The strange language I'd never learned, though it seemed completely familiar to me.

Sliding a random tome from the shelf, I settled into the armchair and flipped the book open. The words shimmered and then settled.

The Watcher's journal

Entry 54163
Watching him isn't my charge, but he is compelling and impossible to ignore, and I know he is hiding something. Where he goes, who he sees, is a mystery, for it is impossible to follow once he takes flight, not without detection. There are plans afoot that I am eager to uncover. Today our Morningstar paid a visit to the nephilim who will help rid us of our murderer. What they discussed was veiled to me, but the expression on Lucifer's face as he left the meeting sent a shiver down my spine. Are the other Black Wings aware of these visits? Should I make them aware? No. My duty is to keep a record of what I see, and that is what I shall do.

Entry 54164
Arthur is dead and the nephilim that ended his life has fled into the night. I have searched to no avail; he has vanished. But I suspect our lord knows of his whereabouts. Did he not visit the night before the act was committed? Was a plan of escape hatched then? The weapons, which should have fallen into Black Wings' care, are gone also. There is a plan afoot that I do not understand. Maybe it is time to reveal my recordings to the others. To make them aware of Lucifer's subterfuge and urge them to demand

answers.

"What do you have there?"

Malphas's voice startled me, and the book slipped from my grasp and to the floor. He bent to retrieve it, a gentle frown marring his forehead.

"The watcher's diaries." He closed the book. "Unless you read Latin, this book is no good to you."

My mouth parted to tell him that sure I could read it, but instinct had me snapping it closed again. There was no point giving away too much information, not if this tidbit might help me escape somehow. It was unlikely that the ability to read a dead language would help, but knowledge was power.

"It looks pretty." I pointed to the book. "The cursive writing is pretty."

He sighed. "Yes, I suppose it is." He walked off into the stacks and returned empty-handed a minute later. "Come. Let me take you back to your room."

I followed him out of the room and into the corridor beyond. The watcher had been talking about Merlin. Lucifer had met with Merlin and plotted something, but what? Lucifer was gone and so was Merlin. Coincidence? I doubted it. There was a connection. Maybe Lucifer knew where Merlin was? Maybe he'd even helped him escape with the weapons? But why not just hide the weapons himself, unless ... unless he had. What if Lucifer had run off with the weapons, leaving everyone to think they were in Merlin's possession? Urgh. My head ached. And what did it matter to us now, anyway? They were gone. The weapons were gone, and we'd been left fighting a centuries'-old battle. Best to focus on my own predicament. Best to focus on getting the heck out of here.

For the next two days, I was either in Abigor's company or Malphas's. There was no chance to plot, or think, or plan. When I did retire to my room to rest, the key scraped in the lock, and I was trapped once again. But each day, my mental map grew.

On the evening of the second day, I unfurled the map and studied it from every angle, growling in frustration when I came up against road block after road block. The ocean was my only escape, but the balcony was a sheer drop down to lethal jagged rocks that jutted out of the water like eager teeth. The only way out of this room was by air, and, unfortunately, I didn't possess a pair of wings.

The hours ticked by and my agitation increased. There was no option but to admit no one was coming for me. No one had told the Protectorate what had happened to me. I was truly a prisoner. And escape, if it did happen, would be days, weeks, or maybe months away. It'd be a chance opportunity, a slip in attention on the Black Wings' part, and constant vigilance on mine. How long before they trusted me enough to let me wander about freely on my own? It was unbearable, and it was all because of these damned daggers, daggers that could set me free if only my demon would join with me. Fucking demon.

"Where are you? Come on, take me. Take control or join with me or whatever you need to do to get me out of here."

There was total and utter silence, and Ambrosius's words echoed in my mind—his revelation about the purpose of the demon. Drayton's demon had proven it, and now mine was doing the same—the reason it was silent was because I was safe. I was safe in my clifftop prison, and there was nothing for it to do.

There was no escape.

Malphas brought me my evening meal and a pile of books. He set the tray on the bedside table and the books on the dresser. "Just a few of my favorites."

"Thank you." I couldn't summon a smile. My head ached from going over and over an escape plan that would never come into fruition.

"The food is good. It's chicken. I made it myself." He nudged the tray.

"I'm not hungry." Yeah, I sounded like a sullen teenager, but what did I care what they thought of me?

"I'm sorry. I truly am."

"Are you? My friend is dead, and my other friends don't even know because you won't let me go so I can tell them. And there's no way you'll tell them, is there?"

Malphas dropped his gaze to the floor. "No."

"And you want me to eat, and read, and stay locked up in this pretty cage you have here. Well, I'm not like you. I don't hide and do nothing when shit is going down." I slid off the bed and strode onto the balcony. The silvery rays of the moon spilled over me, caressing, soothing, but I didn't want to be soothed. "You know, I have half a mind to just jump." I climbed up onto the railing.

"Serenity, please." Malphas held out his hand. "Please, get down."

Could I make it? Would I be lucky and miss the worst of the rocks? My demon wasn't like Drayton's. If I was wounded, that would be that. It couldn't heal me, but Malphas could. He could heal me, and he'd be right behind me. If I made it, I'd dive down deep and swim. He couldn't get me underwater, right? Not with those wings.

I glanced over my shoulder. "I'm sorry. You've been kind. But I need to be free." I jumped.

For a brief moment, suspended in time, I was free, and the sea air filled my lungs, sending euphoria rushing through my blood. But the moment was too brief, and the lethal rocks were reaching up to embrace me—to cut and shred and slice.

What had I done? My scream was ripped away by the wind, and then something slammed into me, and a band wrapped itself around my waist. I was rising up, up, and away from the black rocks, and back into the moonlight.

Malphas. Malphas had caught me. But then I saw Malphas's face suspended over the balcony, mouth open in a large 'o' of horror. If he hadn't caught me, then who had?

I twisted, trying to get a look at my savior.

"Hold still, neph."

I knew that voice. Arrogant and cold. Abbadon.

He dropped me on the balcony and Malphas quickly helped me up. The sea air still stung the insides of my nostrils. The rush of falling and the thrill of death still clung to me like the remnants of a waking dream.

Abbadon glared at Malphas, his cerulean eyes glowing eerily in the moonlight. "What is she doing here?"

The door to my room slammed open and Abigor barreled in. He stopped short at the sight of Abbadon.

"What did you do?" Abbadon demanded.

Abigor's expression was immediately smooth and unreadable. "What you should have done when you had the opportunity."

Abbadon lunged at Abigor, grabbing him by the collar and yanking him forward until they were nose to nose. "You're a fool. An idiotic fool. She was safe with the Protectorate."

"Really? Because when I found her she had a broken arm and had just escaped from The Breed."

"Escaped. She had *escaped*. Don't you see? The daggers are protecting her, and when they cannot, then Bane will certainly do so. But here she is in terrible danger. Not to mention the fact she was almost killed. If I hadn't been returning at this very moment ..." He released Abigor, his lip curling in disgust. "She isn't safe here."

Abigor frowned. "What are you talking about? She is in the midst of Fallen. She could not be any safer. We can give her a room without windows."

Abbadon stepped back, hands on hips. "You think the White Wings do not watch us? That they do not have spies in Midnight who report back our every action?"

Abigor snapped his mouth closed, his eyes shifting from side to side as he made some connection that I was clueless about.

"Oh, Lord," Malphas whispered.

"Yes, take the lord's name now, Malphas. I am disappointed you did not insist she be returned immediately. You are, after all, my second in command. But it seems you have grown soft."

Malphas shook his head. "If the White Wings discover we have kidnapped a nephilim, and that she is staying here with us, then they will question why. They will test and probe and there is a chance they will discover the existence of the daggers."

"It is why I left her to Bane in the first place, although I made it seem as if it were his choice to keep her."

"I am certain that we were not seen," Abigor said.

"Except by the kelpie I summoned," I pointed out. My heart was racing. Did this mean what I thought it meant?

Abigor waved a hand. "Kelpies are nephilim, and they belong to us."

"I must take her back." Abbadon reached for my hand just as a whirlwind of muscle and rage landed on the balcony.

Bane.

He was here. On the fucking balcony, and man, he looked pissed. My body acted on autopilot, rushing toward him on instinct, knowing exactly where it wanted to be. He gathered me up into his arms, holding me to his side protectively. His huge bat wings flexed at his back, but he didn't fold them. He was ready to take off, ready to escape with me.

Abbadon held up both hands. "I was about to return her, Bane. I swear it."

I inhaled his scent. It smelled like home.

"Harker?" Bane asked.

I opened my eyes. "Yes. Abbadon was planning on bringing me back."

"Where's Drayton?" Bane asked.

I tensed. "The Breed had us. Drayton didn't make it." I'd tell him everything, just not here, just not while the Black Wings watched. My chest burned with the shame and guilt of it.

Bane's body shuddered, and his arm tightened around me. "I thought I made my position clear the last time your henchman tried to take her."

Abbadon's jaw clenched. "It was an error in judgment."

Abigor stepped forward. "We all want the same thing. We all want to protect her. And if you were doing a better job of it, I wouldn't have needed to step in."

Bane's muscles flexed around me. "Did he hurt you?"

There was silence. Oh, he was speaking to me again. "No. He didn't. My arm was broken and Malphas healed me. Aside from holding me against my will, they've been kind."

Bane's throat bobbed. "You touch her again, and I will tear your wings from your body. Am I clear?"

Abigor's eyes narrowed. "Do not presume to speak to me that way. You are a nephilim, nothing more than an errand boy, you — "

"Enough, Abigor!" Abbadon ordered. "You were wrong. We had a deal and you broke it. Apologize to Bane. Do it now."

Abigor's nostrils flared, his gaze seared a path across my face, and then he slammed out of the room.

Bane pulled me close. "The wind is high. Wrap yourself around me and hold tight." He hoisted me up, and I clung to him, not caring how intimate the position was. Instead, I reveled in the beat of his heart against my chest and the thud of his pulse against my face. And then we were airborne, and I could finally breathe.

We were going home.

The lounge fire crackled as the flames danced,

casting eerie shadows on the wall. There was silence in the room following my story — absolute, utter silence. And then Cassie began to sob softly. Orin cursed under his breath and Ryker slipped his hand into mine and squeezed. Bane had found me by chance. He'd found me with no help from the kelpies. I'd been lucky he'd done a sweep of the coast, lucky he'd flown as far as the Black Wing manor and heard my voice on the wind. And now they knew the truth. They knew that Drayton was dead. They knew I'd killed him, and they knew that even though I'd saved the two kelpies' lives, Killion had broken my arm and left me for dead.

Bane cleared his throat. "You did what you had to, Harker. No one here blames you for what happened."

"He's right," Orin said. "I blame Max. We can't let this go unanswered. We can't let Max get away with this. He murdered Drayton. He put Harker in a position to have to..." His words choked off. "Drayton was one of us. He was family."

I blinked my stinging eyelids but kept my gaze fixed on the coffee table. "We need to go back. We need to find Drayton and bring him home."

Rivers stood up. "I'll grab a team and head to Desert Rock. See if we can find the entrance, see if I can find him."

I made to stand. "I'm coming with you."

"No." Bane pressed a large hand to my shoulder, holding me down. "Rivers can handle this. You've been through enough."

He didn't want me to see Drayton again, to see what I'd done to him. I squeezed my eyes shut and quelled my arguments, because the cowardly part of me, the part where my nightmares were born, didn't want to go back either.

"They'd have sealed it by now," Ryker said. "They know Serenity and the kelpies escaped. They're probably expecting them to come back with reinforcements. But Drayton ... They may have left him behind." Ryker's throat bobbed. "I'm coming with you."

Rivers nodded curtly.

Ryker released my hand. "I'll be back soon." He pressed a kiss to the side of my head and then followed Rivers out of the room.

Cassie stood up.

"Where are you going?" Orin asked.

"To see Killion."

Orin made a sound of exasperation. "What the fuck is wrong with you? He tried to kill Harker."

She focused her teary gaze on me and caught her bottom lip between her teeth. "I'm sorry, Serenity. I really am. I just ... I have to make sure he's all right." She blinked back tears. "Maybe I can find out what happened to them? Why The Breed took them?"

"You walk out that door and we're through," Orin said levelly.

Her eyes widened a fraction, and then she exhaled slowly and her expression smoothed out. "I guess we're through then."

She strode out of the room.

Orin dropped his head into his hands.

Bane sighed heavily. "Harker, these came for you while you were missing." He pulled two envelopes from his pocket. "We opened them, hoping for clues as to your whereabouts." He handed me the letters.

One was a thick, creamy envelope with my name in fancy font on the front, and the other was Jesse's handwriting. I shucked the letter out and scanned it.

Dear Serenity,

This is the last time you'll hear from me. Not because I'm mad at you, because I'm not, not anymore. I get why you said what you did, why you acted so horribly toward me. You were trying to protect me. I want you to know you don't have to worry anymore. I'm silvered. You've found your place and now I've found mine. I'm happy here. I finally feel safe and at peace. Please be happy for me.

Your sister,
Jesse

It took the words a moment to sink in, then a yawning chasm opened up inside me. She was gone. Truly gone. She'd joined the ranks of the silvered, tipping the scales toward humanity's loss. I'd seen the fervent light in her eyes on more than one occasion when the White Wings had been mentioned. I'd noticed her excitement every time the silvered had walked amongst us. Maybe if I'd been permitted to stay with her, she'd have resisted the call, and maybe she would have caved regardless. It didn't matter.

"I need to get her back."

Bane blinked down at me.

"I need to get into Dawn. I need to get her out."

"You read her letter," Bane said. "She made a choice."

I jerked my arm from his grasp. "A choice to give up all choices. Ever. She doesn't know what she's doing. She doesn't understand. I need to get her out. There has to be a way to get her out."

Bane's eyes narrowed as if he was contemplating something, and then he shook his head. "I'm sorry, Harker. There is no way. Dawn is airtight and in lockdown. To attempt to breach their district would result in serious backlash for Midnight."

My heart sank.

"You must respect your sister's decision."

I screwed up the letter and flung it at the flames. "Fuck this. Just fuck it all."

Orin sighed. "I'm sorry, Harker."

"Open the other envelope," Ryker said.

I snorted. "What more bad news could I possibly get?"

But I did as he suggested and slid the card from the cream envelope. It was an invite to the house games—a reminder of my deal with Dorian. There was a letter inside.

Dear Miss Harker,

The House of Mort has agreed to allow you to take part in the games. The rules are simple. Collect more flags than the House of Vitae and survive the seventy-two hours.

I look forward to your demise.
Dorian

The anger pulsed and then receded a fraction. Yes. I had to win the games and save humans. I had to keep my word to the blonde girl in Dorian's clutches.

Bane plucked the card from my fingers. "I'll speak to him and set this straight."

"No." The word fell softly from my numb lips.

"You need to get some rest," Orin said.

"No." Louder this time. "I need to train for the games."

"Harker…" Orin sighed. "Let Bane deal with this."

I stood up, my body stiff. "Drayton is dead. My sister is gone, and there is nothing I can do about those things. *Nothing*. I can't help them. I can't raise Drayton from the dead, and I can't get my sister back because there is no way into Dawn. But the humans contracted to the House of Vitae do want my help. They *want* to be free, and isn't free will what it's all about?" I locked gazes with Bane.

His eyes narrowed. "Free will?"

"Yes. Free will." I needed him to know that I knew about the test too. I needed him to understand what I was saying. "Isn't it enough that the White Wings are taking humanity's free will? Are we going to allow House of Vitae to do the same?" I took a step toward him, turning my face up to look into his ferocious one. "I can do this, Bane. With your help, I know I can. I *will* win, but I need you to help me." I raised my hands palm-up to expose the undersides of my wrists. "I need you to help me connect with my demon."

He gently grasped my wrists and ran his thumbs over the tattoos. "You've spent years fighting your hunger. Why cave now?"

"Because now I know that accepting my darkness is the only way I can be whole. It's the only way to have control of the daggers. If I'd had control when The Breed took us ..." My voice cracked. "If I'd had control then, I could have cut my way out of the cage sooner, and Drayton would still be alive." The back of my nose and throat stung with the need to break down. "Help me. Please."

Bane's grip on my arms tightened a fraction, and he nodded. "Go get some rest. We'll begin training tomorrow."

Alone in my room, I crawled onto my bed, curled up, and closed my eyes. If I was going to succeed, the dam would have to break. I'd have to remember, and then I needed to move forward.

Drayton's face filled my mind. His horrified gaze sliced through my heart as I plunged the daggers into his ribs. His warm brown eyes filled my mind as he told me to run. I let go, allowing the grief to wash over me. Guilt and sorrow and anger wracked my body.

My fault. Mine.

I'd been stubborn and refused to listen to Ambrosius, and I'd lost Drayton. My body shook with uncontrollable sobs that tore at my throat. I was broken, shattering into a thousand pieces, and then the bed behind me dipped and a warm body enveloped me.

Bane's scent filled my nostrils. He pulled me toward him, my back to his chest. "It will be all right. I promise it will be all right."

"It hurts …"

"I know. But the pain will recede. It *will* get better."

He said the words with such conviction

that a part of me almost believed him, but how could it be true? How could this tumult of guilt and agony ever go away? "It won't. It will never get better. Drayton is dead because of me, and my sister is silvered because I pushed her away."

He sat up. "Get up."

I rolled to face him. "What?"

"Get up and put your boots on. We're going to Dawn."

We flew high above the city, over Midnight and into Sunset, where the warmth of the sun kissed my cheeks like a blessing. My eyes watered, assaulted by the brightness. And then we were sailing close to Dawn. It was dark ahead — real night — because in Dawn, the winged enjoyed both the sun and the moon. The orange rays receded, and I blinked away the moisture, able to see properly again. Bane hung back amongst the mist, where we had a splendid view of the pearly gates. They rose up so high, a short dip would allow us to brush against them even from this height.

"What are they made of?"

"Pearl," Bane said. "It's a material used excessively on the divine plane but one that I find is rare on the mortal one."

Lights scanned the night on a regular circuit. Looking for intruders and keeping watch on the residents.

Bane hovered with me in his arms. "We can't go in this way. The gates are always guarded, but there is a blind spot."

His wings beat at our backs as he rode the wind, keeping a good distance between us and Dawn. We left Sunset behind and were engulfed in the natural night of the White Wings' district.

"Hold tight and stay tucked in," he whispered into my hair.

We were doing this, really doing this.

"One, two, three." He dove.

I bit back a scream as we streaked beneath the beams, up and over, and down again. He flew like a master, taking my breath with every twist and turn of his body and every shift in the air as he changed gears. And then, we were landing softly on the ground.

He didn't release me, but loosened his grip enough to allow me to take in my surroundings. We were tucked into an alley, squashed up against a brick wall. Beyond the mouth of the alley sat a stone well and a cobbled square. An iron post with a lamp on top lit the square with warm light.

It looked like something out of a historical novel. The Victorian era ... Yeah, it reminded me of those paintings and books that I'd pored over in the library. This was Dawn? This was how they lived? It made no sense. They had such power at their disposal. They provided Sunset with electrical goods all the time, and yet they used none here?

I leaned in to Bane. "Why is it so old-fashioned?"

He sighed against my ear. "The White Wings believe that technology corrupts. Ironic, because they use it in the towers overlooking the silvered dwellings. They just feel that humans should live a basic life. Grind their own wheat and sew their own clothes, that kind of thing. Idle hands lead to anarchy, after all." His tone was laced with bitterness.

Jesse had chosen *this* over Sunset. I had to get her out. She obviously had no idea what she was doing. I'd left her, pushed her away, and she was confused, looking for direction in a place that promised security and safety.

"Okay, stick close and remain in the shadow," Bane said. "The fledgling house is across the square."

"How do you know this?"

He exhaled through his nose. "Who do you think helped build this district?"

"Nephilim?"

He nodded. "When we first came here. When Arcadia was first born."

It was the first time he'd openly admitted to knowing of a world outside of this city, of being from the mysterious wide world beyond. There were so many questions …

"Don't. It will only make it harder to live if

you know what it is you are missing. Trust me on that."

"Fine. But why did you help the White Wings build this place if you hate it so much?"

"I don't hate it. It's a way of life, and if some choose it, then so be it. I just don't believe that humanity should be forced into it. That was the whole point of this experiment. It was to show the White Wings that, on the whole, humanity would prefer to be free to forge their own path and to make their own decisions." He held out his hand. "Are you ready?"

I nodded and slipped my hand into his. We set off across the square, running from one pocket of darkness to the next. The small, compact buildings surrounding the well were lit from within with flickering light—candles, no doubt. The fledgling house came into view—a proud three-story affair with grand double doors and three neat steps leading up to them.

A gust of air brushed against my face in warning, and then the flap of wings followed.

"Shit." Bane tugged me all the way across the square and into the alley beside the fledgling building just as two huge White Wings landed in the square.

They flexed their wings and laughed.

"Will she be willing, do you think?" one asked the other.

"It matters not. She must submit to my will."

The other one chuckled. "Mine is enraptured with me. She opens for me with stars in her pretty eyes, and she tastes sweet and fresh."

They slapped each other on the backs. "Fledglings," they said in unison.

My heart stalled and ice filled my veins.

Bane's grip on my arm tightened.

The two White Wings strode right toward us, veering suddenly to climb up the steps to the fledgling house. There was a knock and then light spilled onto the cobbles as the door was opened. The murmur of voices drifted out into the night, followed by more boisterous laughter from the White Wings, and then the door cut off the shaft of light.

I pressed my back to the cold stone. "They're taking advantage of the fledglings."

His jaw flexed. "Bastards."

"Get me to my sister. I need to get her out. Now."

Bane tucked in his chin. "As much as I'd like nothing more than to beat those White Wings to a pulp, we're out of our depth here. We can't go in. Not while they're inside. And who knows how long they'll remain. The longer we linger, the more chance there is of us being spotted. We need to leave. Now."

I'd come this far. I was not leaving her here. "Bane ... Please. Just help me get inside. I can find her and get her out, and then we can fly the heck out of here."

"Serenity, if you're caught …"

"I won't be. I promise."

Okay, so it was a promise I may not be able to keep, but leaving Jesse here at the White Wings' mercy was not an option. If they caught me, then so be it. They'd never know how I got in.

"You can't make that promise, Harker. I'm sorry. We're leaving." He wound his arm around my waist.

"No." I pushed at his solid chest. "I'll scream. I swear if you force me to leave without Jesse, I'll scream."

"I did you a favor, and you repay me with a tantrum?" His eyes blazed in the gloom, and shame unfurled in my chest.

I closed my eyes. "I'm sorry. God. What am I doing? I just … I can't come all this way and not try."

Jesse was alone in the fledgling house, at the mercy of the lecherous White Wings. My bottom lip trembled, and I caught it between my teeth.

"Fucking hell, woman," Bane growled in exasperation, and then looked up, scanning the wall. "There's an open window and a ledge. Climb up onto my back."

He was going to do it. He was going to get me into the building. I clambered up and clung to his neck. Bane began to climb. His powerful fingers gripped the gaps in the stone, and we rose up until we were level with the window. It was an empty bedchamber. A single candle burned, but no one was inside.

"Get in. Do not be seen. Find her and meet me in the alley," Bane said.

Before I could respond, the door opened and a woman slipped into the room. She was dressed in a white nightgown that fell to her feet and was buttoned up to her neck. Her golden hair was loose and fell down her back in gentle waves. A White Wing strode into the room behind her. My pulse jumped and my fingers tightened around Bane, but he was already in motion. He slipped away from the window and hugged the wall beside it while balancing precariously on the ledge. It all happened so fast, but not before I'd seen the woman's face. Not before I knew it was Jesse.

"It's her. It's her and a White Wing has her."

"Shh," Bane cautioned.

Voices drifted out toward me. Jesse's tinkling laughter was followed by the unmistakable sound of making out. My stomach turned. He was forcing himself on my sister, my pure, helpless sister. Why had I sent her back to Sunset? Why hadn't I kept her with me? More voices drifted out of the window, the words too soft to make out, and then the sound of a door opening and closing cut the air. I needed to see what the heck was going on. As if sensing my thoughts, Bane shifted toward the window to allow me to peer in.

Jesse was by the bed, her back to me as she turned down the covers.

She was alone.

"Jesse, over here."

Her back straightened sharply, and she spun around, her eyes going wide when she caught sight of me. She pressed a hand to her mouth and rushed over.

"What are you doing here? You can't be here. You need to leave now."

"Trust me, I'm not staying. We're getting out of here. Now. Put on your shoes."

She glanced at her bare feet then slowly raised her head to look at me with that look—the jutted chin and determined glint. "I'm *not* going with you."

"What?" What was she talking about? "The White Wing will be back any minute. You need to come, before he ... before he ..."

"Has sex with me? Makes my body feel alive for the first time in forever? Yeah, I'm eager to do that." Her words dripped with sarcasm.

"You *want* him?"

"Yes. I *want* him. I love him, and he loves me, and I'm happy here. I've been chosen to be part of his harem. I'm moving tomorrow."

A harem ... "You can't be serious."

Her eyes narrowed. "For once in my life, I

finally have somewhere that I belong. I'm happy here. I fit in, and it's safe. *Please* don't ruin this for me. If they find you here, then they'll expel me. I couldn't bear it. Please. You have to go."

She was crying now. Wringing her hands and glancing at the door, worried her White Wing would come back and catch us.

"Harker?" Bane asked.

This wasn't right. She couldn't possibly be saying what I thought she was. "You're happy being a puppet?"

Her gaze hardened. "Yes. I'm happy. You have no idea how much easier it is not to have to make decisions, to have all the many choices taken away. I feel free."

Free? She had no fucking idea, and the words to shatter her illusion burned on my tongue. I bit them back. Telling her the truth would doom humanity. It would void the contract between the winged.

"You want to stay …"

"I want to." The door knob turned. "Go away." She drew the drapes, blocking us out.

There was nothing more to do here. Nothing.

The journey home was a silent one. Jesse had made her position clear. What more was there to say? We landed on the roost, but Bane didn't release me immediately.

"Are you all right?" he asked tentatively.

The tone was so not Bane. It was too kind and gentle, tugging at the knot that was holding my emotions in check and pulling it loose.

My eyes welled. "No. No. I'm not all right. Did you see the way she looked at me? As if I'd come to shoot her in the head, not save her."

"She didn't want to be saved, Harker. For some people, free will is a burden. An anchor they will happily relinquish."

"Then why? Why do we fight to preserve it?"

"Because it is a gift from the Creator. One that every human has the right to, whether they want it or not."

Jesse had chosen to give up this gift. "She's gone. Truly gone."

My chest heaved with sobs and his arms tightened around me, a barrier against the pain, a safe zone in which to vent.

"Let it out, Harker. Just let it out. And then pick yourself up and meet the next challenge. Because tomorrow is another day. There will always be another day."

Ryker's soft voice tugged me from the blissful oblivion of sleep, and, for a moment, I forgot what had happened. I forgot about Drayton's death and Jesse's rejection, but then it hit me, and the pain came flooding back. My breath caught on a gasp. No. No more grief. No more tears.

"Serenity?" Ryker stood by my bed.

I rolled onto my back, into the heat and imprint left behind by Bane. My neck heated. I'd asked him to stay, to hold me until I fell asleep. Fuck, how the heck had I found the nerve to do that? And he'd done it. He'd stayed. Somewhere along the way, a line had been blurred.

Ryker was studying me carefully. "Bane left to go speak to Dorian about a half hour ago."

His words were like a bucket of ice, and I was up like a shot. "What? Why? He promised to help me. He said I could compete in the games."

Ryker gave me a small smile. "Yes. And Bane honors his word. He's gone to renegotiate the terms. House games are a team sport, and it's only fair you get a team of your own."

Did he mean what I thought he did?

"We're going with you, Harker. Bane and I. It's only fair. The other houses will have teams of six each. Technically, we'll still be at a disadvantage, so Dorian shouldn't be too put out by the suggestion."

A bitter taste rose up in my mouth. "Bane thinks I won't survive solo."

"Do *you* think you will?"

I pinched the bridge of my nose. This wasn't about my ego. This was about the humans I'd vowed to protect. "I honestly don't know."

"Bane and I will be just as clueless as you when it comes to these games, but together maybe we can come out alive."

Alive, not victorious. He really didn't think we had a hope of winning.

"What did Rivers find?"

"Nothing. Just as I predicted. In the absence of a body we're going to hold a small private ceremony to say goodbye to Drayton. Orin is organizing it for after the games."

Drayton was truly gone. Jesse was gone. I closed my eyes and took a deep breath. No more dwelling. It was time to make things happen. "What's the plan for today?"

"Cassie never came back. I'm going to the coast to speak to the sea riders," Ryker said. "I thought you might like to come."

"How long have I been out?"

"You slept through. It's nine a.m."

"Okay, give me ten and I'll meet you in the foyer."

He left me to wash and dress. My eyes were puffy from all the crying, but the water was ice cold and took away the redness and inflammation. I pulled my auburn hair back into a French braid, slicked on some gloss, and applied some kohl. I needed to look badass and feel badass. My little excursion with Bane was never to be mentioned to the others. He'd made me promise. It made me wonder why. Why had he taken such a risk for me? He'd said he took care of his own. Maybe this was his way of showing me that. Dropping the line of unproductive thoughts, I headed out of my room to meet with Ryker.

Ryker hovered by the front entrance, his axe strapped to his back. He looked up as I climbed down the stairs, stood up straighter, and then nodded curtly.

It was time to get some answers.

It was barely ten thirty, but The Deep was already busy. The music was low and the floor was taken up by tables where patrons were drinking coffee and eating breakfast. The nightclub had been transformed into an eatery, and servers rushed to and fro with platters laden with delicious crispy bacon, eggs, toast, and some stuff I'd never seen before.

Jonah raised a hand in greeting as we entered, and Ryker made a beeline toward the bar. "Have you seen Cassie?"

Jonah jerked his head to the left just as a flurry of laughter filled the air.

Killion and his sea riders were firmly ensconced at a table up against the wall. He had his arm around a female whose back was to us, but that fiery red hair was unmistakable.

Ryker sighed. "Let's get this over with."

For a Protectorate member, he really wasn't

big on conflict. But he wove between the tables, passing nephs and humans who looked up curiously to see an axe-wielding neph so early in the morning.

The laughter died as we approached, and the kelpies facing us nudged each other. Cassie went to turn around, but Killion's arm tightened around her neck.

"Cassie?" Ryker said. "Can we have a word, please?"

Killion slowly slid his arm from her shoulders and turned in his seat to face us. "Cassie is busy right now."

Cassie kept her back to us.

"Are you seriously going to let him speak for you?" Ryker asked her.

Cassie's shoulders rose and fell, and then she slung an arm over her seat and half turned to look at us. "I'll be back for patrol, okay. That's all you need to know."

Her dismissive tone, her don't-give-a-fuck expression, were like fuel to the fire inside me that was desperate to burn up shit.

"You know what, Cassie, if you want to stay and suck on Killion's cock, that's fine. We didn't come here for you. We came to speak to *him*." I jerked a thumb at Killion. "You owe me, fishy. I saved your life, and even though you left me to die, I'm here, alive, and ready to collect."

Killion didn't even blink. There was not even a flash of guilt on his impassive face. The guy must be some kind of sociopath. Instead, he picked up a toothpick and stabbed at his teeth. Long seconds passed, and I was about to erupt when he spoke.

"What do you want?"

"I want to know exactly what happened underground. Why did The Breed take you? What did they want?"

His left eye twitched. "I already told Cassie."

"Yeah. Well, unfortunately, she didn't relay the information."

Cassie tucked in her chin.

Damn her, what was wrong with her? "Drayton is dead because of The Breed, and all you can think about is getting cozy with your ex? You need to get your priorities straight."

Her head whipped up. "He's dead because *you* killed him. Maybe if you'd stopped being such a whiney bitch and learned to accept your cambion nature, none of this would have happened. You have daggers that can cut through anything. You could have escaped before they drained him of power."

Killion sat up a little straighter. "What was that about daggers?"

Ryker shot Cassie a lethal look. No one was meant to know what the daggers could seriously do. If word got out, then The Order would come looking. The daggers were enchanted objects, and The Order was all about the magic.

Her face flushed. "Nothing. Look. Just go. I'll be back later. I want to be here."

I ignored her and focused my attention on Killion. "What did The Breed want from you?"

He sat back and graced me with a slow blink. "They wanted our bliss. They extracted it from the others. Cut out the gland that secretes it. They killed them to get to it. We were meant to be next, but you came and let us out."

"And you broke my arm as a thank you."

He shrugged. "You survived. It seems like you're a tenacious thing."

God, he made me sick. "Why would they want your bliss?"

"How should I know? You'd need to ask them, and if you do manage to get hold of one of them, then I would appreciate an invite. We have a score to settle."

"That's it? You're going to sit back and do nothing?"

He picked up a fry and popped it in his mouth. "It's not my job to do anything. It's yours."

My hand itched to slap his smug face, but that would mean touching him. There was nothing more for us here. I turned away in disgust. "Let's get out of here."

There was no doubt in my mind that I'd get my revenge on Max. I'd make it my mission to find the leader of The Breed and hurt him. But now, it was time to train. Train and become the darkness.

Ryker had gone to hunt for Bane. The boss would need an update, and we needed to know if Dorian had agreed to our fresh terms. But my thoughts were with Orin. He'd been devastated the night before when Cassie had left, and the fact that she hadn't returned was probably tearing him up. He deserved to know the truth. He wasn't in his room or the training room. The study was empty and so was the lounge. God, I was an idiot. I knew exactly where he'd be.

Orin was pulling a tray of scones out of the oven when I entered the kitchen. He placed them on a cooling rack and then took off his apron. "Would you like one? They're delicious when hot."

Damn, he was grief baking. "Sure. Thanks."

He popped one on a plate and handed it over. "Butter?"

"I'm good."

He leaned back, his hands braced on the counter, head hanging. "Did you see her?"

The scone no longer looked so good. "Yeah, I did."

"Is she all right?"

"She seems fine."

His shoulders rose and fell. "I guess that's all I can hope for." He sniffed. "What did she … did she say anything?"

He deserved to know the truth, so I told him what she'd said and how she'd acted. "She said she'd be back for patrol."

His shoulders began to shake.

Oh, man. Was he crying? Had I ever seen a man cry? No. No, I hadn't, and seeing Orin break down like this tore at something deep inside me. I shoved my seat back and rounded the table.

He looked up as I approached and wiped at his eyes. "Fuck, you must think I'm such a pussy."

"No, Orin. I think you're one of the strongest guys I know."

I wrapped my arms around him and laid my head on his chest. He tucked his head into the crook of my neck and broke down. I held him for an age, making soothing circles on his broad back. Finally, his sobs subsided, and he raised his chin to rest it on top of my head.

I patted his back. "You're going to be

okay."

His chest rumbled. "I know. And so will you."

My eyes pricked and I blinked back the threat of tears, plastered a smile on my face, and gently pulled away to look up at him. "Now, how about we eat some scones. You got jam?"

He matched my smile with a watery one of his own and then pressed a kiss to my forehead. "I got jam."

Ryker hadn't materialized by the time Orin and I polished off the scones, and so I went in search of him.

Serenity. Thank goodness you are safe.

I paused in the corridor leading to the steps to the third floor and Bane's domain. My chest tightened with fury I'd been holding back, and for a moment it was impossible to form words.

Serenity?

"Where did you go? Tell me where you went. I want to know now."

I cannot.

"Then fuck off and don't come back, you hear me. I don't need you. I don't need secrets and unpredictable alliances. I need honesty, stability, and people I can count on."

You can count on me, Serenity. I promise I will not steer you wrong.

"But you weren't there. You weren't there

when I needed you." Fuck's sake, I was getting teary again. I hated this. *Hated* it. "I needed to master the darkness. I needed to save Drayton and you were silent."

I'm sorry.

"Sorry? Great. That's fucking great. Who the fuck are you anyway? Why the heck am I even listening to you?" Something clicked in my mind, a piece of the puzzle I'd been subconsciously putting together, and gooseflesh broke out on my skin. "You're him, aren't you? You're Merlin!"

With Malphas's revelations clear in my mind, the connection was obvious. Even without everything he'd told me, I should have made this connection sooner. Merlin had created the daggers. Maybe this was him communicating with me somehow. It made sense. Malphas had said that Merlin vanished after Arthur died, and the only things he'd left behind were the daggers. Why forge them and leave them? They served a purpose; there was no doubt about that. And maybe Merlin was somehow linked to them.

"Are you Merlin? Answer me. And don't you dare give me some cryptic, bullshit response."

Ambrosius snorted. *If only that were true. I am merely a construct. I am the consciousness he gifted to the daggers. A guide for whomever they were to choose. Your guide. And I promise that you can count on me.*

"You know where he is, don't you?"

My question was greeted by silence. Damn him, he wasn't going to answer. I strode up and down the corridor, struggling to bring the anger back under control. "Okay, so you're a guide, huh? For what? Answer me. What am I being guided toward?"

When the time is right, then all will be revealed.

God, I wanted to smash something. "You're so lucky you're a disembodied voice, because if you were here in the flesh I'd have punched you by now."

I'm sorry, Serenity. I do not mean to upset you. If I could tell you, I would, but the words are locked away until the time is right.

What choice did I have but to accept what he was saying? He'd saved my life and, so far, hadn't steered me wrong. "Fine, then guide me now. Teach me to assimilate."

I wish I could. But you've blocked your demon for so long I wouldn't know where to begin. The only thing I can suggest is to leave your shields open and allow her to get to know you, to bond with you.

"And how long will that take?"

I don't know. Weeks, months.

"Cannot say, don't know, what good are you?"

God, I was being a bitch, but I didn't care. I needed this. I needed to rage and vent and blame anyone but myself for what had happened.

It will take time.

He faded away, leaving me alone and cold in the aftermath of my ranting.

There was no way I was waiting weeks or months to become whole. Even without the daggers, there was power in the darkness, power within the demon, and I wanted it. I needed it. And I would have it. Bane. I needed Bane.

My knock went unanswered, and still on a high from the adrenaline Ambrosius's visit had flooded my body with, I entered Bane's chambers.

It was dark. No moonlight, just a couple of bedside lamps. The bed itself was unmade, as if Bane had just climbed out. A book lay open but face down on a wingback by the window. There was no sign of Bane.

Where the heck was he?

I was about to leave when a door to my left clicked open and Bane ducked out, huge, muscular, and totally naked.

"Oh, fuck!" I spun around and slapped my hands over my eyes.

There was a long beat of silence, and then, "Did you want me, Harker?"

Want him? What? Oh, yeah. "I wanted to ask what Dorian said."

The rustle of fabric teased the air. Thank goodness he was getting dressed.

"He had little choice. If he declined, he would have looked like he didn't have faith in his chosen representatives."

The band around my chest eased slightly. Of course, I'd have gone solo if need be — that *had* been the original deal — but I was no fool. Having Bane and Ryker along would make the task seem less daunting.

"Okay, good."

"You can turn around now."

I faced him and swallowed the lump in my throat. He'd covered up his legs and his ... stuff, but his chest was still awesomely bare.

I averted my gaze. "Ambrosius says it could take weeks, even months, to become one with my demon."

"You want a faster solution." His tone was a low rumble that had the hairs on the back of my neck standing on end.

"There has to be something we can do? Do you know anyone who might be able to help me?"

He was silent for so long I couldn't help but look at him. He'd tucked in his chin, hands on hips.

"Bane?"

"This is important to you? The only way you can be whole?"

"Yes."

He locked gazes with me. "In that case, I know someone."

I exhaled in relief. "Thank you."

He nodded. "Leave it to me. I'll make arrangements. Meanwhile, find Ryker and get warmed up for some training. Focus on stamina and hand-to-hand; we're going to need it. I'll be with you in half an hour."

I slipped out of his room, leaving him to his thoughts, and headed off, eager to find Ryker and begin the training.

Bane held me tight, but not so tight as to bruise. "Remember what I taught you."

It was our fourth training session and the techniques the guys had been drumming into me were finally beginning to stick. I twisted and used my momentum and body weight to flip him. He hit the mat and rolled back up.

"Not bad." He flashed fang. "Not bad at all."

I was breathing hard, sweat pouring down my back, but he looked cool and unaffected. We'd been at this for a couple of hours. Hand-to-hand maneuvers. Ways I could get away from a larger opponent, that kind of thing, and damn if I wasn't sweating like a pig in a sauna.

Bane stepped back and cracked his neck. "Let's try the pin position again."

My pulse lurched. But I lay down on the

mat. This one was hard, more due to the distraction factor than anything else. Bane straddled me and pinned my arms to the mat with his huge hands. I was completely at his mercy. The heat of his body, his scent, and his inner thighs pressing against mine combined to turn my head to mush and awake a thrilling carnal hunger. The urge to touch him, to be touched, was almost a physical pain. Focus, Harker. Time to turn it into aggression. I bucked and writhed.

"Lead with the leg, hook, and turn," Bane said. "Come on, you can do this."

I twisted under him, rubbing up against him, biting the insides of my cheeks to quell a throaty moan. "You're too heavy."

"Yes. I'm heavier than you." He leaned in, his face inches from mine. "I've got you. I'm in control. I can do whatever the fuck I want to you, so what are you going to do to stop me?"

His words sent a thrill through me, part fear, part desire. Oh, God. I hated this exercise.

"Stop me, Harker." His breath fanned my lips, and then he adjusted his grip so he was pinning both my wrists with one hand. "Stop me." His other hand slipped down to tease the edge of my slacks.

My body tensed and then began to buzz with crazy energy. He tugged gently on my slacks. He was giving me a chance to act, because I was meant to be stopping him. Shit.

Okay. Concentrate on the move. Raising my knee, I slammed my outer thigh into his inner thigh, raised my hips, and turned my body. He toppled to the side, and I was up.

"Finally." He pulled himself up. "You should go shower and change. Lilith will be here to help you with your demon soon."

"What?"

He swallowed and averted his gaze. "She'll be here in a couple of hours."

Lilith was the person who could help me? Of course, it made sense, she *was* a succubus—the original, if legend was to be believed—but the thought of working with her on anything had my stomach turning with nausea.

There'd be a price with her. I just knew it. "What does she want in return?"

His expression shuttered. "What makes you think she wants anything in return?"

Because I see the hungry way she looks at you. "Because she's a bitch."

Bane's lips twitched. "Maybe so. But she's the only one that can help you, and we will pay what we must to give you what you need."

Great. "What do I need to give her?"

He walked away toward the benches. "*You* don't need to give her anything."

I didn't … wait … "No. Not you."

He grabbed his water bottle and glugged. "Don't worry, Harker. I'm a big boy. I can take care of myself."

Then why was the skin around his eyes so strained, and why were the violet depths filled with darkness?

Sod this. "No. We are not doing this. I can wait. I'll just let it happen naturally over time, like Ambrosius said."

"It's too late. The deal has been struck, and she arrives shortly."

Panic squeezed my lungs. "Then un-strike it." The thought of her getting her claws into him, of making him do things he didn't want to … I walked up to him and grabbed his arm, forcing him to look at me. "Please, just tell her we changed our minds."

"Don't forget who's in charge here, Harker," he snapped. "I don't take kindly to my decisions being questioned."

I flinched at his harsh tone but held my ground. "Then maybe it's time you got used to it."

"And maybe it's time you remembered who the fuck you're talking to."

We stared each other down for a long beat, and then he exhaled heavily, the tension draining from his massive shoulders.

He shook his head and reached out to tuck a strand of my hair behind my ear, his fingers lingering a fraction too long. "I can handle Lilith." His tone lowered. "Don't worry. Just use what she has to offer."

His hand was still hovering at my cheek,

and I reached up to partially cover it with mine. The words weren't spoken, but they were there, hovering between us—the memory of what I'd seen, what he knew I'd seen out in the forest. "I can't bear it."

"Then I will bear it for the both of us." He slipped his hand from beneath mine, and the warm, open expression withdrew and closed off. He turned away. "Go get showered and rest. I have no idea what she has in store, but no doubt it will be draining."

Lilith was coming and she'd want Bane's body as payment. Bile rose up in my throat. I couldn't let him do that, not for me. There had to be another way to give her what she needed.

And then a light bulb switched on in my mind.

I knew what I had to do to protect Bane.

I paced the lounge, hands on hips. Lilith was due to arrive any moment. According to Bane, she owned several properties in Midnight, and sometimes even vacationed in Dawn. The succubus had clout, and she'd probably never go for my plan, but I had to try. It was bad enough that Bane had to endure her attentions every few months due to a deal he'd struck with her. There was no way I was making him go through another session just for me. If she agreed to my terms, then we'd work together. Otherwise, she could piss off back where she'd come from.

Bane appeared in the archway, and the clip of heels alerted me to the succubus's presence. She glided into the room, brushing up against Bane in the process, and came to stand by the hearth, less than a meter from me.

"Well, well. I see you've finally acknowledged your problem," she purred.

I clenched my teeth and forced my lips into a smile. "*Can* you help me?" Or are you just here to gloat.

"I wouldn't be here if I couldn't." Her lips curled in a sly smile as she gave Bane a sidelong glance. "Besides, the price is more than worth the journey."

This was my cue. "Yeah. About that. I want to renegotiate."

Her eyes narrowed. "Oh?"

"Yes. You still get your sexual energy, but you get it via a middleman."

She made an 'o' with her mouth. "So, the rumors are true. You can not only siphon, but you can expel the power into another."

"Yeah. I can."

The corner of her mouth quirked. "How perfectly, wickedly delicious." She paused and pouted. "Wait, so you wish to create the sexual energy with Bane, and then expel it into me?"

"Harker, what are you doing?" Bane said.

I shot him a hard look. "Shut up."

He opened and closed his mouth, and Lilith burst out laughing.

"Oh, my." She pressed a red-taloned finger to her crimson lips. "This is interesting. It takes gumption to negotiate with me. I like it. It's … refreshing." She clapped her hands together. "I agree to your terms."

I blinked at her in shock. "Really?"

She laughed again, a sexy, sultry sound.

"Yes, really. Why shouldn't I?" She shrugged. "I get the benefit without any of the work. Although, I do enjoy our time together, Bane."

Bane's gaze was a hot brand on the side of my face, but I couldn't look at him right now. I was still reeling from the relatively easy win.

"Now, shall we get acquainted with your demon?" Lilith indicated the sofa. "Have a seat."

I parked my butt and waited as she hitched up her pencil skirt and crouched in front of me. This close up, you'd expect to see some imperfection, a pore or two, but her skin was smooth, flawless, and unblemished, almost as if it had been carved out of marble. Her lashes were thick, long, and uncoated with mascara. There was no softness to her features, just harsh lines and cold planes. Hers was a cruel beauty.

She cupped my face, tilting my head this way and that as she examined me. For what, who knew?

"We need to coax her out," Lilith said. "Bring her into the forefront of your consciousness. I can do that for you, but then it is up to you to convince her to remain."

"Convince her?"

"Why, yes. You must speak to her. Tell her why you have kept her a prisoner for so long, and beg for forgiveness for your mistreatment of her." There was a flash of anger in her dark eyes, and a needle of fear slid up my spine.

My mouth was dry. "I didn't do it

maliciously. I didn't know what I was, or what I was dealing with."

The spark of danger evaporated, and she sniffed. "Yes. Well, that is something you must take up with your demon. Now close your eyes and relax." Her fingers dug into my skull. "Come out, my child. Come to Mother."

My darkness unfurled and began to rise. I'd felt her all my life but never like this—larger than life and almost tangible.

"Serenity, let go," Lilith said.

Let go? Let go. And then I was falling into my mind, losing grip on the world and tumbling into her—into my darkness.

"Hello?" It was cold here—cold, misty, and gloomy. "Is anyone there?"

"I'm always here. I'm always there. I'm always everywhere."

That voice? It was raspy and rough, but it was mine.

It was anticipation that made my pulse flutter. "Come closer. I need to see you."

"Not yet," the demon said. "First tell me why you have come. Why acknowledge me after so long?"

Was I standing? Was I sitting? It was impossible to tell. "We need to talk."

"Isn't that what we are doing?"

"I didn't know. I didn't understand what you were."

"*Are*, not *were*. You didn't want to

understand. Not really."

Okay. "Maybe you're right."

"Of course I'm right. I know you. Every part of you."

"Have you heard me calling you?"

"Yes."

"You didn't answer. You're angry with me."

"Yes."

"Is that why you didn't help me? Why you didn't join with me when I called to you?"

"Partly, but mainly because you cannot be trusted." The voice vibrated with suppressed rage. "You use and then you lock away. You feed, but then you starve. I protect you because I must, not because I wish to."

Oh, God. Shit. She was mega pissed. "I'm sorry. I'm so sorry. If I'd understood what you were …"

"You would still have locked me away. You locked me away to play at being human. You are ashamed of me. Of us. But now … Now, you want me. Now you want me to be you and you want to be me." The voice was moving, circling me.

"Yes. Yes, I want you. I want us to be together, to be whole. I know I don't deserve it. I know I've hurt you, but if you'll forgive me, I promise I'll never shun you or push you out again."

"Never?"

"Never."

"Your solemn vow."

"I give you my vow."

She was silent for several agonizing beats. "I accept your vow. I will join you."

"So, what now? What happens—"

A twisted, dark thing leapt out of the mist and smashed into my mind. I was being torn, shredded, and invaded, and the burn was brighter than a supernova. I glimpsed the light just for a moment, shimmering pure and powerful. It was the light from the lake—the light in my dream. And then I was staring into dark eyes—Lilith's eyes—and the world was bright and sharp and new.

"There you are, little one," Lilith said. "And what is that?" She probed deeper, pushing into my mind, and my demon reared up and smacked her back.

Lilith released me with a surprised chuckle. "Feisty." She dusted off her hands, stood, and sashayed over to the drinks tray. "Well, I can say with confidence that was a success."

Did I feel different? I stood and looked inward. My shields were down. But where was the darkness?

"Where is it? Where is my demon?"

"Inside you, where it's been all along. You *are* the demon now, Serenity. It is truly a part of you. It is your flip side and your protector. She will come to the forefront when needed, when you call. You will have control."

The daggers. I needed to know if I could will them into being. But Lilith wasn't in the know about those enchanted objects, so I clenched my fists. "I need a minute." I strode out of the room, up the stairs, and onto the landing. Taking a deep breath, I stared at my hands. Daggers, please. Was that a chuckle in my mind? My hands stung and then the daggers appeared.

It had worked. It really had. "Thank you."

A sigh.

The thought crossed my mind that I no longer needed the daggers, and they vanished. I'd done it. With a little help from Lilith, but still, I'd done it. My demon was finally a part of me, and it was time to pay the piper.

A shiver of anticipation went up my spine—not me, so not me.

It was my demon.

"You don't have to do this," Bane said softly.

We were up on the roost, in the chill air, back where we'd kissed for the first time and created sexual energy to feed to Drayton's demon.

Drayton.

No, don't think about him. Focus on Bane. Bane needed my help.

"I'm sure."

He slipped his hand around the back of my

neck, his fingers sliding through my hair. "She may not be satisfied with what we have to offer."

There was real heat in the violet depths of his eyes, real want, and my heart rate picked up. Yes. I wanted this. I wanted him. It was my voice, yet not my voice. It was strong, hungry, and eager. I pressed myself against him, reveling in the hard planes of his body, exhaling and inhaling to prepare for what we were about to do, what we were about to create. And then his lips met mine, and I was on fire. He kissed me like I was the last woman on earth, as if his heart would explode if he stopped to take a breath. Instead, he breathed me in. But his hands, his hands he kept to himself. It was sweet torture because I wanted him to touch me, I needed him to. I tore my mouth from his.

"More. We need more." I grasped his hand and placed it on my breast. "Touch me." My voice was lower, harsher.

It wasn't mine.

Bane closed his eyes. "Serenity. If I start, I may not be able to stop."

My heart lurched and my core grew liquid. "I'm willing to take the risk."

His hand closed over my breast, thumb sweeping back and forth over my nipple. My breath caught in my throat, and a low, ragged moan spilled from my lips. His mouth descended on mine, and this time, he wasn't holding back. He hoisted me up and slammed me against the wall, trapping me with his body as he devoured me. Yes. This was what I needed, what I wanted—the power, the sweet, electric power. It coursed into me, filling me, making me melt and writhe and moan.

"Harker ... Fuck me ..." Bane's voice was thick with desire.

I stared at him from beneath heavy lids. More. I needed more.

He pulled away, his eyes bright, his expression dazed. "I think we have enough."

His words were like a dunking in the sea. What the heck had I been doing? He lowered me to the ground and stepped away, taking his heat with him. *Touch me*. Had I said that? God. My cheeks heated and laughter filled my head.

Bane turned away from me.

Yeah, this was the dark side getting its own back, all right.

"I'll ... I'll just go deliver." I hurried for the door.

He remained with his back to me, his shoulders rising and falling erratically. "Yeah, do that."

Lilith set down her glass as I entered the lounge. Her eyes lit up. "Well, that was quick. He must have really been ready to explode if he came that quickly."

Came? Oh, shit. Did she think we'd had sex? Is that what she was expecting?

She tiltled her head. "You did fuck, right?"

I cleared my throat. "No. We didn't need to. We just happen to produce a ton of sexual energy just by kissing." My tone was cocky, sassy, and I liked it.

Her expression hardened. "That wasn't the deal."

"Yes, it was. No one said anything about sex."

Her lips thinned. "Fine. Give it to me."

I strode over to her, grabbed her by the back of the neck, and pressed my lips to hers. She opened under the pressure, and the power I'd generated with Bane came flooding out of me and into her. It was over quickly, thank goodness. I wiped my mouth with the back of my hand. Urgh, her lipstick was all over me. Yuck.

She ran a finger over her lips, her eyes bright with ecstasy. "Now that ... that is something."

"I'm glad you enjoyed it. Now you can leave."

Her brows shot up. "Demon suits you. I like it." She clipped past me into the hallway just as Bane appeared. He zoned in on my lipstick-smeared mouth and then on Lilith and grimaced. I shrugged to indicate it hadn't been too bad.

"That was some hit, Bane," Lilith purred. "Thoroughly satisfying." She trailed a hand across his chest as she passed. "I'll see you in a few weeks."

My stomach tightened. "Take your time. Don't hurry back."

She left on a peal of laughter.

Bane walked toward me, reached up, and ran the pad of his thumb over my mouth, his lips turned down. "I'm sorry."

What was he apologizing for? For letting go of me up on the roost? For stopping. Or for my having to kiss Lilith. Neither of those things mattered.

"It's all right."

Ryker walked into the room followed by Orin and Rivers.

If they were all here then ... "Who's on patrol?"

"Orin and I are just on our way out," Rivers said. "Bane wanted to see us."

Bane tore his attention from my mouth and transferred it to the other Protectorate members. "The Breed took bliss from the kelpies, and we need to find out what they need it for."

"Shit," Orin said. "That stuff is potent."

He knew about bliss? "How do you know what bliss is?"

"Descended from sea dwellers, remember. You hear things. And the kelpies' bliss has always given them an edge over other predatory sea dwellers."

"Yes, it's powerful stuff," Bane added. "And it only works on humans. We need to find out what The Breed intend to do with it and when they are planning to strike. They're beneath us. Underground. We assumed the network of tunnels had been etched by Arachne, but, upon reflection, we may have been wrong."

"You think it's been The Breed's hideout all along?" Ryker asked. "That Arachne was merely squatting?"

Bane shrugged. "I don't know. And we can't exactly ask the huge spider. She's sealed up behind brick and stone, but someone, somewhere in the city, will have to have heard or seen something. Scope out the hidey holes. The drug dealers, the illegal export and importers. Speak to the lowlife, and see what you can dig up."

Rivers nodded. "On it." He glanced at me, then back to Bane. "Is everything all right?"

Bane snorted. "Why don't you ask her yourself?"

Rivers looked to me. "Harker?"

"I'm fine. It went fine."

He nodded. "If you need me …"

Bane tensed.

I offered Rivers a smile. "Thank you."

The boys left the room and Bane followed. "Get some food and some rest. Tomorrow, we see what you can really do."

Showered and fed, I climbed into bed. Sleep was close, whispering in my ear. *Serenity. Serenity, you did it. You did it.*

Wait, that wasn't sleep. That was Ambrosius. "Yeah. I did it."

How?

"Lilith helped."

He was silent for the longest time. *She was here? She touched you?*

The memory of my mouth on hers came to mind. "Um, just a little."

Did she see the dagger tattoos?

"No."

Good. Keep it that way.

That was the plan, but my curiosity as to why he wanted me to keep the secret was piqued. "Why can't she know?"

Because she cannot be trusted. Ever.

Yeah, well, I could have guessed that.

There was something off about that woman, aside from her energy-sucking ways. She had a rotten core.

This is good. This means you are almost ready.

"Ready for what?"

He was silent for a long beat. *For the house games, of course. Now you can enter with confidence.*

"I thought you were against that."

You are whole now, Serenity. Learn what that means, and you will be fine.

"Whole and confused. The demon seems to have a habit of projecting her feelings onto me."

What do you mean?

I sighed and shifted to get comfortable. "I kissed Bane to siphon sexual energy, and she was a little too eager, if you get what I mean."

He laughed softly. *The demon is your wants and desires reflected back at you and amplified. You need to feed, and so it gives you hunger. You need to be safe, and so it protects you, and you wanted to be with Bane, and so it gave you that too.*

Hang on, what was he implying? "No. I was ... I had feelings for Drayton."

It is possible to desire more than one person. To be drawn to different partners for different reasons. In our world, there are more gray shades than black and white.

"I want Bane?"

It seems that you just might.

What was I to make of that?

Rivers found me in the kitchen loading up on protein before my scheduled late morning training session. I scarfed the last sausage and washed it down with tea.

I jerked my head toward the skillet on the hob. "You want some? I made plenty."

He sniffed the air. "The smell led me here. It does look good."

"Thanks."

"Why aren't you on dinner duty?"

I held up my hands. "Hey, if you want breakfast for dinner, then great. This is about the extent of my expertise."

Rivers's eyes crinkled at the corners. "I suspect you have many skills, Harker. I suspect you could do anything you set your mind to."

The compliment coaxed a warm flutter in my belly. "Thanks, Rivers. That was sweet."

His lips tightened. "Just a fact. Drayton would be proud of you. The way you're training so hard for the games and your determination." He dropped his gaze and pressed his lips together. "But I think you're making a mistake."

"What?"

"It's too risky. You could be killed."

"Bane and Ryker are coming with me. I'll be fine."

"Neither of them know what to expect, not really. What if you get split up? What then?" His brows were drawn low over his aquiline nose, and his slender face was etched in concern. "You could die."

I nodded slowly. "Yes. I could. I could die choking on a piece of sausage, or fall asleep in the bath and drown. Life is filled with risks. Living in fear of death is not true living."

He flinched as if I'd slapped him.

"What?"

He shook his head, a small smile playing on his lips. It wasn't even a proper smile, but it lit up his face, turning the studious, harsh features into something compelling. My pulse skipped a beat. What had I said?

"You remind me of someone I used to know. She was a lot like you in many ways." He held up his hands. "Looks like I have no choice but to help. I know Bane and Ryker have got you covered with training. But if you need anything else, then I'm here for you."

Was he talking about Ryker's dead sister? The one Cassie had told me about? Was I really that much like her?

"I appreciate that, Rivers, and I may take you up on your offer."

He nodded curtly, walked over to the dish rack, and grabbed a plate. He glanced over his shoulder and frowned. "Don't you have training to get to?"

***

The obstacle course stared at me tauntingly. "Are you fucking serious?"

Bane stared at me impassively. "Do I look like I'm fucking joking?"

Ryker choked on his water. "Bane, that's not very inspirational."

Bane rolled his eyes and exhaled heavily. "You can do this, Harker. You have your demon. Trust the power." He delivered the lines in a monotone.

Damn, someone was in a bitching mood today.

I exhaled slow and long and jumped up and down on the spot. "Okay. I'm going to do it."

"Today would be nice," Bane drawled.

"Just focus, Serenity," Ryker said. "Visualize the course. Visualize overcoming each obstacle, and then let your instincts guide you."

Yeah? The jumps were high, the ropes way too far apart, and the ledges sliver-thin. How the heck? Okay, are you there, demon thing? Can you hear me? A shift in my mind, as if another pair of eyes was looking out from behind mine, using me as a window. A sense of confidence flooded me, slow and easy and sure.

I set off at a run and sailed over the first hurdle, rolled under the next, and leapt for the rope, landing over halfway up. My fingers stung and my nails elongated, wicked sharp.

What the heck?

My demon laughed, and then the talons slid back into my skin. Swing, swing, swing, leap, the sliver of the ledge was beneath me, and, shit, I was balanced on it like a fucking ninja. Damn. Now to stand and run. I was doing this. Ooh, how about a flip to finish off? Could I do a ... Yep, I so could.

I landed in a crouch. I did it. I bloody did it, and I wasn't even winded.

A slow clap filled the silence, and I turned to see Ryker with a huge grin on his face.

Bane remained impassive. "Not bad. Now, let's get serious." He drew his sword. "Get your axe, Ryker. We're going to take Harker and her demon for a spin."

Doubt crossed Ryker's face. He still didn't think I could handle this, and, for a moment, his doubt pierced my armor of confidence, but my demon reared her head and smacked me down.

This was possible.

Ryker and Bane circled me.

My daggers appeared. Relax, focus, relax. Let your instincts and your senses guide you. I exhaled and closed my eyes.

Ryker and Bane's attack was signaled by the whoosh of air, and my body moved to counter. I was spinning, acting before I could think, *chink, slice, chink, slice.*

"Fuck!" Bane said. "That was my favorite

sword."

I opened my eyes to see him holding up the hilt of his broken sword. My dagger had cut straight through it. His horror was real and his face was just too comical.

Ryker snorted and then began to laugh.

His axe was split too, one half of the head sliced completely off, but he didn't seem bothered. He was too busy clutching his abdomen and doubling over laughing. His mirth was infectious, damn it. My lips were twitching, and then I was joining him with a howl of my own.

Bane glared at us from beneath thick brows. "You think this is funny?"

"Yeah," Ryker said.

"You should see your face." My laughter died. Drayton … Drayton had said that to me all the time. "That's enough training. I'm ready. I got this."

My daggers retreated, and I strode from the room before they could see me cry.

My room was my haven for the next fifteen minutes, where I allowed myself to remember him, where I broke my promise and grieved a little more. Deep breaths, okay. You can do this. Cold water washed away the burn of the tears. I walked out of the bathroom to find Ryker leaning against my door frame.

I sniffed. "What happened to knocking?"

"Come on, let's go grab a bite."

"We're going out?"

"Yeah. Fresh air will do you good."

I was willing to try anything. "Let me just grab my coat."

We parked on a side street and walked the short distance to the corner cafe lit up bright and welcoming in the perpetual darkness. Tiny stores lined the street. We passed a used book store and a couple of antique furniture shops and then a small jewelry store. My feet faltered as something caught my eye in the window. It glinted invitingly from the window display, but on closer inspection, it was a simple item—a silver pendant in the shape of a tiny snowflake. It was pretty and unique.

"What are you looking at?" Ryker asked.

I pointed to the pendant. "It's pretty."

"We can come back when the store is open."

"Sure, but for now let's get that grub you promised."

Leaving the pretty trinket behind, we crossed the street toward the eatery.

The cafe was a cozy affair filled with humans enjoying a meal. It was late, almost half eleven, but the humans here were wide awake and enjoying the night.

"You'd think they'd be tucked up safe at home."

Ryker laughed. "Most of the humans here belong to a house. They have protection, and the scourge isn't meant to run for another week. They're safe enough."

We slipped into a corner booth. "Why do you think the scourge is acting so weird? You think it's something to do with The Breed?"

"I don't know, but I have this feeling. This horrible feeling that something awful is coming."

"Isn't that Cassie's forte?" I couldn't keep the bitterness out of my tone.

"Don't be too harsh on her."

"Seriously? After the way she's acted and the way she's treated Orin?"

"Orin is a grown man. He knew what he was getting into when he started seeing Cassie. He knew where her heart lay, however misguided it may be. But that's not why I'm asking you to back off."

"Then why?"

"Cassie is a banshee, or is meant to be. It's always been her thing. It's how she's contributed to the team. But for the past year or so, she's been off. Her feelings, her warnings of danger, have either come too late or not at all, and the other day, with Drayton and you, she blames herself for not sensing something sooner. When we found the battered car, she was beside herself. She spent every waking moment combing the district for clues as to your whereabouts, and then to find out Drayton was dead... It's probably all been too much."

Shit, now I just felt, well, shitty. "I wish you'd told me all this before we went to see her. I'd have been less bitchy."

He picked up a menu. "To be honest, it didn't really occur to me until much later. I was so mad at her too." He pressed the menu to the table. "The waffles here are great."

"Waffles it is, then."

A young woman came over and took our order.

A few minutes later two mugs of coffee appeared.

Ryker took a sip and sighed. "I needed that. Are you nervous?"

"Yes."

"Good. You should be. Never get complacent. Never take anything for granted."

"Yes, sensei."

He snorted into his coffee.

I handed him a napkin. "Wipe your face, you're embarrassing yourself."

He mopped up, shaking his head, and then his expression sobered. "How are you coping, though? Really?"

He was talking about Drayton. How was I coping with Drayton being gone? "I'm good. Just focusing on the house games."

"But the games won't last forever."

I puffed out my cheeks and blew out a

breath. "I know, but I'll deal with that when the time comes."

"And Bane?"

My head whipped up and my cheeks heated. "Look, I had no choice. I was not letting Lilith get her claws into him."

He slid a hand over mine. "I know. Believe me, I get it. And it's all right to give a damn."

I pinched the bridge of my nose. "I just need this to go right. I need to beat the Sanguinata."

"You will. I promise you." He leaned in, his baby blues intense. "Listen to me, Harker. I promise you that I will protect you out there. I will not let any harm come to you." He blinked and dropped his gaze. "Before Drayton died, he came to me. He was mad because he thought... he thought ..."

"I had romantic feelings for you."

His eyes widened. "You knew?"

I winced. "I may have overheard your conversation."

His throat bobbed. "Do you know about my sister?"

I fingered my coffee mug. "I know you had one. I know she died, and I think I might remind you of her."

He closed his eyes. "Pretty much." He sat back in his seat. "It was a long time ago. Sometimes, it feels like she was just a dream. If not for the small mementos of her, I'd begin to believe she only ever existed in my imagination."

"How *did* she die?"

"Painfully. I wasn't there to save her. Decades ago, when we first began to protect humanity, there were no districts, no treaty, and many nephs—like the sea dwellers, the Lupin, and Sanguinata—fed off whom they pleased. Giselle was a fierce warrior, a champion of humanity and ferociously protective of them. Humans flocked to her. They adored her for her compassion and kindness. But the nephs who wanted to have free reign didn't like that. There was a faction back then called The Supremacy. They believed themselves to be better than humans, better than other nephs. It was The Supremacy that killed her." He picked up his coffee and took a huge gulp. "Rivers was with her when she was taken. He fought them, but he was unable to stop them. They disabled his weapon—his voice—using a specially made torque. He was unable to fight back the way he would have."

"With his voice?"

"Yes. With his siren ability, Rivers could have convinced them to stop. To walk away. He could have convinced them of anything, and he could have disabled them with a shriek that would have made their brain explode. But he was powerless. They forced him to watch her be tortured." He exhaled through his nose. "They sent her back to us in pieces."

"Oh, God." I grabbed his hand and squeezed.

"Rivers they left alive, as a cruel joke. He was almost catatonic when we found him. He made little sense, and he was unable to tell us where they'd been held. But you see, the joke was on them. A few nights later, Rivers went back. He'd lied to us. He'd lied about not knowing, and he went back alone and unleashed his voice."

"He killed them?"

"Yes, along with half a block of human residents."

My hand flew to my mouth.

"He didn't care. He didn't care for a long time, and when he finally surfaced, he was a wreck. Did you notice the silver shackle on his wrist?"

I nodded.

"It's a muter. His punishment to himself for besmirching Giselle's memory by killing all those humans she'd loved."

"I'm sorry. So sorry you lost her like that."

He smiled sadly. "And then I saw you walking into the Protectorate foyer and it was as if she were walking toward me. And when you were exiled to Midnight, I knew then that I was being given a second chance. I said to myself: Ryker, you need to keep her safe. And I almost failed. You could have died underground.

Twice."

Oh, man. He was putting himself into the role of my guardian. It was a role that didn't belong to anyone but my demon. "I'm not your responsibility. I'm your teammate, your equal, and your friend. And even though I may remind you of her, I'm not Giselle. You do not need to watch over me, and frankly, if you did, I'd have to punch you."

"Serenity, I—"

I held up a hand. "Let me finish. I may get into scrapes, but they're *my* scrapes, and I have my demon to watch out for me, not to mention two awesome daggers to cut the shit outta anyone who messes with me." The daggers materialized on cue. I winked and they vanished. "So, promise me you'll stop stressing."

He exhaled. "Teammates."

"Yeah, teammates."

A commotion broke out at the front of the cafe. The server arrived with our food and slid the plates quickly onto the table.

Ryker twisted in his seat to look at the entrance. "Is there a problem up there?"

The woman wrung her hands. "Members of the Order of Merlin. They come by from time to time trying to recruit."

Ryker slid out of the booth and I followed. We walked toward the front of the cafe, and the commotion died down. Four Order members stood by the doors dressed in black, tight-fitted combat gear with cloaks draped over their shoulders. Three of them were new faces, but the woman I recognized.

Marika.

"So, you crawled back to Midnight, after all," Ryker said.

Marika ignored him and focused on me. "Hello, Serenity Harker. We've been looking for you."

"Me?"

She smiled, and it was probably meant to be a warm gesture, but it failed to penetrate her eyes and left me feeling uneasy.

"We just want to speak to you about your pretty dagger tattoos. It won't take long." She jerked her head. "Outside. Away from the fragile humans."

My skin broke out in gooseflesh. How could they have ... Fucking Killion and his big mouth.

Ryker leaned in. "Four more outside."

I nodded. "What choice do we have?"

If we stayed indoors, we risked getting into a scuffle that could hurt the human clientele.

I donned a nonchalant air. "Sure, mind if I get my waffles to go?"

Marika arched a brow. "Be my guest."

I turned to the woman who'd served us. "Can you bag up our food, please?"

She nodded quickly and hurried off.

"Shit, my coat." I went after her, back to

the table. She was picking up the plates. "When we leave, call the Protectorate. Tell them Harker and Ryker have been taken by The Order."

Her eyes grew round.

"Can you do that?"

She nodded.

"Thanks." I grabbed my jacket and waved the server away. "You know what. Forget the waffles. They'll just get cold, and I hate cold waffles." I sauntered back up to Ryker. "Shall we?"

Heart pounding like a drum, we stepped out into the night. The street was empty save for The Order and us. They surrounded us, with Marika taking point.

She licked her lips. "Can I see them? Can I see the tattoos?"

I crossed my arms. "No."

She sighed. "Look. I just need to confirm what they are."

"And what do you think they are?"

"Something ancient and important. Something that belongs with The Order."

"Really? Then why the fuck aren't they hanging out on an Order member's skin?"

She blinked in surprise at the vehemence in my voice.

"Here's a newsflash for you: not everything magic is your property."

She looked taken aback. "Is that what you've been told? Is that what *they've* told you?"

She raked Ryker over with disgust. "They would say that."

"Hey. I'm one of them."

"No." She shook her head. "You're not. You can't be. If the daggers chose you, then you, Serenity Harker, are one of us. Come with us and let us enlighten you."

I rolled my eyes. "No, thanks."

She pressed her lips together. "Aren't you curious as to what they are? Aren't you curious as to *why* they've chosen you?"

Damn it, of course I was, but not enough to go anywhere with her. Not of my own free will anyway. The Black Wings had warned me about them, Ambrosius had warned me, and so had the Protectorate.

"Well? Aren't you?" she pressed.

I shrugged. "Nope. And I'm not going anywhere with you. So, you may as well piss off."

This was it. This was when they'd attack. Ryker tensed, ready to take on whatever. His hand twitched to draw his axe.

Marika massaged her temples. "Fine." She withdrew something from her pocket and handed it to me.

A card. A business card with her name and number printed neatly on it. What the heck?

"We're not your enemy, Serenity. Trust me. You'll realize that soon enough, and when you're ready for real answers, then call me." She raised a hand and made a swirling motion in the air with her index finger. The Order turned away and strode off into the night.

"Ryker, what the heck just happened?"

He shook his head, his mouth parted in shock. "The world is going insane."

A screech of tires had us leaping back to avoid collision with a black van.

The Protectorate van.

Ryker looked to me in confusion. "What are they doing here?"

"Oops."

The tall electrified fence stretched far to the left and right. For this event, Bane had agreed to have his wings bound. Rivers had placed a strange silver clip at Bane's back, pinning his wings so it was impossible to unfurl them. Flags had been hidden by a human force employed by the council for impartiality. The whole event was moderated by them to ensure a fair outcome.

This was our entry point. The House of Vitae and the House of Mort had their own. The plan was to get in, establish a base, and then get to work finding the flags. Ryker was responsible for setting traps. Bane was the muscle, and, with my newfound agility, I was the flag snatcher. This was my chance to turn things around. I'd failed Drayton and Jesse. I would not fail the humans relying on me to win.

The human moderator cleared his throat. "Are you ready?"

"Get on with it," Bane snapped.

He cleared his throat again and flipped the switch to open the door in the gate. It shuddered and whirred and then we were through. We stepped onto a huge stretch of land filled with forest, streams, abandoned buildings, and goodness only knew what kind of traps set by the opposition.

Forest land lay to our right, and to our left were rolling hills.

"Head for cover," Bane said.

We bolted for the trees. It was even darker under the canopy of leaves, and the silence was thick and heavy.

"We need to find somewhere to set up base," Ryker said.

"Follow me." Bane set off, his steps sure in the dark.

I kept close to his broad back, not wanting to lose him in the dark. "It's almost as if you know where you're going."

Bane snorted. "This land wasn't always used for the house games. It's been here for almost a century, and the house games are merely thirty years old."

"So, you're familiar with the terrain?"

"Yes. I'm familiar. This forest land is dense. It covers most of the land. There's an abandoned mansion east from here. It's probably surrounded by an overgrown garden now. No doubt the Sanguinata will claim it, if possible.

There's a groundsman's lodge to the west that the Lupin will enjoy."

Wow. "I'm glad you came."

He shot me a grin over his shoulder. "Just be grateful Dorian's arrogance prevented him from figuring out I'd have an advantage."

We wove through the trees, quickly, stealthily. "Where are we headed then?"

"There's a cabin up ahead, just over the stream."

The sound of running water reached my ears, and then a stream came into view, shallow and rocky and easily crossed. The forest seemed even denser on the other side, and we had to fight our way through the tangle of branches and brambles.

"Are you sure about this?" Ryker asked.

Bane made a sound of exasperation and forged ahead. "Be careful, don't damage the branches. It will make it easier for them to track us here." And then we stumbled into a clearing, well, as clear as you could expect in the unkempt wilderness. A tiny log cabin covered in moss sat at the center.

The door was stiff but opened with a shove of Bane's shoulder, and then we were inside. It smelled musty and slightly damp.

Ryker crouched by the dusty hearth. "I'll get a fire going."

"No," Bane said. "Do you want to announce our whereabouts?"

"It's fucking freezing? How do you suggest we stay warm?"

"Body heat," Bane said.

Shit, he was good. I would have built a fire without even questioning it. Wait, did he just say body heat?

"Don't look so stricken, Harker," Bane said lightly. "Everyone likes snuggles."

Ryker made a choking sound.

Had he just said snuggles? What the heck?

Bane's lip twitched, and then he strode off to examine what would be our base for the next seventy-two hours. Every time I thought I had a handle on this guy, he switched things up. Just when I got accustomed to his snapping, he soothed things over, and when I got used to the lack of humor, he threw in a pun.

Ryker jerked his head toward the door. "Harker, let's scout the perimeter and set some traps to alert us to intruders."

The next two hours were spent helping Ryker roll out trip wire and tangle bells in the bushes to alert us of anyone coming or going. He'd arrived well stocked, his backpack bulging with strange items. We laid down spike mats, covering them with leaves and twigs, and even set up an alarm system. When we were done, he flicked his wrist to make the air shudder around each trap to test that it worked.

"How do you do that?"

He shrugged. "I don't know. I just do. I feel

connected to the air, as if it's a friend."

"I wonder what Aether is."

"What calls to you?"

"The energy inside others." The answer tripped off my lips. "You think it's something to do with energy?"

"Everything is some form of energy. You're not like the regular incubus who feeds off one kind of energy. You seem to be able to pick and choose. Maybe that's the key. I'm sure we'll find out eventually."

"Yeah, it hardly matters with my ninja moves, right?" I nudged him with my shoulder.

He rolled his eyes. "Or your big head."

"Hey, my head is the perfectly perfect size for my body."

He looked me up and down. "Annoyingly true."

Perimeter secure, we headed back inside, where Bane was fiddling with some kind of machine he'd set on the rickety table.

"A generator?" Ryker rushed over to take a look. "Damn it. We need Rivers for this shit."

Bane played with some wires and then flipped a switch. The generator made a strange chugging sound and then began to hum.

Bane stood back. "Now we're cooking. Or we will be once I get this plugged back in." He carried the machine to the kitchen area and opened the cupboard under the counter. Five minutes later, we had light.

"Turn them off," Bane said. "Harker, there are candles and matches in the drawer over there."

They were huge, chunky things. I lit them but kept them in the center of the cabin.

Bane tested the two-ring hob. It worked, which meant hot food. We'd brought cans of soup and beans and some scones that Orin had packed. It would do for the seventy-two hours we'd be stuck here.

We were ready to hunt for flags.

An hour and a half later, we'd scouted two miles around the perimeter of the base, and were about to admit defeat, when I spotted the prize. Shining silver in the moonlight, the flag was tied to a high tree branch.

"I got this." I took a few steps back and then launched myself at the trunk. My nails elongated, jamming into the bark, and I was off, scrambling up like a marsupial on speed. Damn, it felt good. From up here, the forest was laid out before me, and far to the east, the rolling plains bathed in silver were visible. The flag was in my hand, then clutched between my teeth, and I was about to make a break for the ground when movement caught my eye. Shapes loping close to the ground and headed this way.

The Lupin. It had to be.

Shit. Time to shimmy my arse down to the

team.

Back on the ground, I tucked the flag into my jacket. "We need to move. We have incoming."

"Did they see you?" Bane asked.

"I don't know. But if I saw them, it's highly possible that they saw me."

We took off back the way we'd come, moving fast. "Wait!" I ground to a halt. "We can't lead them back to base. We need to split up and throw them off."

Bane nodded. "You head to base, and I'll create a diversion."

"No. I'm faster. I'll lead them off track and double back and meet you guys."

Ryker looked ready to protest. But Bane nodded. "Do it."

I spun on my heel and ran back toward the danger.

Howls cut through the air. The Lupin were on the hunt. Wolf men, Ryker had said. Men who could tear you to shreds with their teeth and claws. It would be my first encounter, and, yeah, I was happy to skip it. I skidded to a halt by the tree where the flag had been and waited. They were getting closer. I needed to hold off. Let them catch my scent and then run.

The next howl was so close I almost felt its vibrations.

Time to run.

I cut east, leading them away from base.

This was new terrain, but my mental map was on, taking in all the details and storing them away for later use. Shit, a flag. Damn it, no time to stop and grab it. It was high up again. I'd double back and get it later. The Lupin were at my back—their paws scraping earth as they ran, eager to cut me down. Another howl, and I took a sharp left, leading them farther off course. And then a new sound rose up into the air—the sound of a horn, low, ominous, and loud.

Shit. It was close by. Who the fuck was that? More Lupin? Or was it the Sanguinata? My body was suddenly sheathed in perspiration, part exertion, part fear, because at my back were the howls, and in front of me was the horn.

What to do?

Acting on instinct, I leapt up into the nearest tree, right to the top where the canopy was thick and would hide me. If they sniffed me out, I was fucked. But the howls and the horn were set on a collision course, and, hopefully, the horn was Sanguinata and they'd end up fighting amongst themselves. I crouched, clung, and waited. Less than a minute passed, and the Lupin crashed into sight on the forest floor. There were three of them, which left three unaccounted for because Ryker had said the houses had teams of six.

The horn sounded again, and the Lupin skidded to a halt a meter away from my tree. They were huge, buff guys, but way too hairy for my tastes. Their arms hung a little too long, and their haunches rippled with power. They were also naked, their bits on display for all to see. Big bits.

The one closest to the tree growled, "What the fuck is that?"

"Fucking Sanguinata playing tricks, no doubt," one of his companions said.

"Let 'em come, pasty motherfuckers," the third member of the trio said. "We took them down last year, we can take 'em down again."

He was the smallest, in more ways than one, but his swagger was the largest. Compensating much?

The horn was super close now, and then there was something else. The sound of hooves. It sounded like ... horses.

The Lupin backed up a step, suddenly wary, and the temperature dropped, leaving my breath a mist in front of my face. This was not the Sanguinata; this was something else. They rode onto the dirt track straight at the Lupin — black mist and crimson fabric. Laughter rose up to meet me — triumphant and hungry — and then the screams began.

My hands were frozen claws digging into the tree as my eyes tried to make sense of what I was seeing — riders on horseback moving fluidly. They were ethereal one moment and flesh the next. The Lupin fought, but their claws slipped through shadows, which immediately solidified to a whip or a sword that cut into their hairy hides.

Fresh ground.

Fresh meat.

Fresh hunt.

Their words echoed in my mind, and then a shadow stopped and looked up—looked right at me with its abyss eyes. My lungs stopped working, my brain froze. It saw me. It had me. There was nothing else but this connection as it slowly cocked its head as if considering, as if musing whether to climb up and rip me from my perch. And then it turned away, melding into the mass as they began to ride again. They ran west, thank goodness, away from our base.

The Lupin lay in tatters, their bodies ripped open with weapons they couldn't counter.

I needed to get down. I needed to get back to base, back to Bane and Ryker. I needed to warn them, but the thought of leaving the sanctuary of the tree made my chest tighten in panic and turned my bowels liquid. Move, Harker. Bloody move.

Bloody.

So much blood.

Inch by inch, heart in my mouth, coppery tang on my tongue, I climbed down the trunk. My feet kissed the ground, and I ran.

"Tell me what you saw again," Bane said. "Take it slow."

I recounted my tale for the third time, and, yes, it sounded just as ridiculous this time around. "There's something out there. Something that isn't Sanguinata or Lupin. Bane, we need to get out of here. It isn't safe."

His mouth twisted wryly. "Being here was never a safe option."

"Yes, but at least we knew our enemy. We had a fighting chance. There is no fighting these things. Not if you can't touch them."

Ryker paced the cabin. "The other Lupin will come looking for their teammates, and when they find them dead, they'll be pissed. They'll scour every inch of the forest, and they will find our base."

He was ignoring the most important fact. "That's the least of our worries. What if the shadow riders find us first? Look, this isn't about flags and dodging the houses anymore. A fourth player has entered the game, and we need to warn the others."

"You want to actively go looking for the Lupin and Sanguinata?" Bane asked.

"The plan was to find the flags and stay alive," Ryker said.

What was wrong with them? Why weren't they taking this threat seriously? "Are you listening to me? There is something out there that should not be here. Something powerful and dangerous and ..." They were walking away, talking amongst themselves and completely ignoring me.

I slammed my hands on the table and stood. "What the fuck is wrong with both of you?"

Bane and Ryker turned to me in surprise.

"Harker, calm down," Ryker said. "Whatever is out there, we can handle it. We've been doing this for a long time. Trust us."

"You can handle shadow riders who you can't actually touch?"

He was staring at me blankly again.

Something was wrong; it was as if my words were going through a filter and the urgency and danger was being stripped from them.

Bane placed a bowl of soup in front of me. "You did good today, Harker. We got our first flag, and tomorrow we'll get more. We'll hit the south side of the forest. There are some ruins we can explore."

They walked off, chatting amongst themselves again. Yep, there was something terribly wrong. For some reason, they just weren't grasping the urgency of the situation. In fact, the more time that passed, the less concerned they were.

Was I being overly cautious? Had I really seen what I thought I'd seen?

The memory of the terror was still vivid. I'd have to convince them, but it was becoming obvious the only way to do that would be to show them what we were up against, and that thought chilled me to the bone.

"Are you warm enough?" Ryker asked.

"Yeah. Toasty. You guys are like portable heaters."

On the other side of me, Bane chuckled. "Most neph tend to run hot."

"Most except me."

Ryker was facing me but Bane had his back to me. We'd lined up our sleeping bags against the wall.

Was it weird being sandwiched between them? Yep. Was I going to try and change the sleeping arrangements? Nope. I liked being warm. And this was super cozy. The sleeping bags took the edge off lying on the floor, and with Ryker and Bane's solid walls of muscle on either side of me, it was like being in a safe cocoon.

I nestled down into my bag. "So, what's the plan for tomorrow?"

"More flags," Bane said. "I have a hunch the ruins will have one, maybe two. I doubt the Lupin or the Sanguinata have made it that far."

"How far is it?"

"Half a mile."

"And what if we come across the shadow riders?"

Bane was silent for a long beat. "Who?"

Was he kidding me right now? "The shadow riders I told you about."

He rolled over to face me. "Serenity, I have no idea what you're talking about."

He was deadly serious. I rolled onto my back to look up into Ryker's face, which was just as confused as Bane's. They didn't remember or had mystically been forced to forget. But why could I still remember what I'd seen?

I smiled, but my lips quivered. "It's fine. I'm tired. Let's just get some shut-eye."

I ducked under the covers, heart pounding. What the fuck was going on?

I woke up pressed up against Bane's chest with Ryker pushed up against my back, his hand resting on my hip. Two sets of morning glory said hey. Yep, pretty awkward. Bane opened his eyes and just stared at me. His pupils were huge, sucking me in, and the heat of his hardness was suddenly a searing brand across my thigh. My hand was resting on his chest, and the only evidence that he was affected by our intimate position was a slight acceleration in his heartbeat. He didn't move away immediately, he didn't even apologize, but then why was I surprised? Bane didn't do apologies.

But Ryker did.

"Shit," Ryker muttered before backing away from me as if he'd been burned. "Fuck. Harker. I'm sorry."

Bane snorted and rolled away, taking his heat with him. "Relax, Ryker. She knows you didn't mean it."

But Ryker wouldn't look at me and what I could see of his face was tinged pink.

Wait. What had Bane said? She knows *you* didn't mean it, not *we* didn't mean it.

I glanced across at him, and he turned away on a slow blink. My pulse throbbed heavily in my throat. The neph was dangerous and unpredictable, and it both thrilled and frightened me.

Bane pulled on his boots and rolled up his sleeping bag. "Get up, get dressed. Let's go hunt some fucking flags and win this thing."

The ruins were an overgrown mess. Stone

was netted with ivy, and weeds sprouted everywhere between. The plant life seemed to be in competition to see who could claim more of the structure. This place had been a mansion once, but what was it doing in the midst of the forest? The tree line was close, barely leaving enough room for any kind of grounds, and there was no official path to this place.

"What is a mansion doing smack bang in the middle of the forest?" Ryker asked.

Bane's mouth lifted. "It was beautiful once. A hideaway for the reclusive." He sighed. "It's simply a cavern of memories now."

The nostalgia in his tone tugged at my curiosity, but the shiver of apprehension that had been with me since we'd left the cabin was stronger.

"Let's just find the flags and get out of here."

We crunched closer, emerging out of the tree line into the moonlit space where the dilapidated mansion stood, eyeless and morose.

Figures spilled from the left and the right. Four of them. Sanguinata.

"Looking for these?" a tall figure to the left said. He held up two flags. They gleamed dully.

"Shit," Ryker said.

Bane's chest rumbled. "Thank you for retrieving them for us."

Ryker slid his axe from its sheath at his back.

The Sanguinata fanned out.

"Is this the little neph with the grand designs?" another Sanguinata asked.

"The very same," his companion replied. "And you know what Dorian wants, don't you?"

"Yes, to save her till last."

"Fresh meat makes for a better transition."

They were talking about Dorian turning me. Yeah, like that was gonna happen.

My daggers materialized in my hands, and I raised them. "Well, what are you waiting for, boys? Come and get me."

"Where the fuck did her daggers come from?" the fourth Sanguinata asked his companions.

But Bane, Ryker, and I were advancing. It was time to rumble.

Rumble ... The ground was shaking, accompanied by the sound of hooves. The blast of a horn followed.

The Sanguinata's heads whipped around to the left, toward the sound.

"What the fuck are the Lupin playing at?" the one I'd identified as their leader asked.

I lowered the blades. "Not the Lupin. It's the shadow riders."

Bane made an exasperated sound. "Harker, what the fuck are you talking about?"

I backed up. "You need to run. All of us need to run. Now."

The clearing exploded with sound and

shadow as the riders swarmed in.

"Oh, God." Ryker grabbed my arm and pulled me back toward the tree line, but Bane stood silent and frozen, his gaze fixed on the mass as it attacked the Sanguinata.

Like the Lupin, there was no way for them to counter the attack, and their screams were horrific as they were torn asunder.

Bane took one step back, then another, before spinning on his heel. "Run!"

The three of us and the Sanguinata leader made a break for it. I took the lead, angling away from the cabin. The Sanguinata was fast, running abreast of me. Shit, he was almost as fast as me. If it had been them I'd come across yesterday, and not the Lupin, they may actually have caught me.

We ducked low-hanging branches and leapt over roots. The unmistakable sound of rushing water warned us about the river before we barreled onto the bank.

"I don't think they're behind us," Ryker said.

The Sanguinata glanced back into the trees. "What the heck was that?"

I caught my breath. "I saw them yesterday. They killed three Lupin."

"And you didn't think to warn us?" Bane snapped at me. "You do realize this isn't part of the game, right?"

My demon cursed, and I placed my hands

on my hips and glared at Bane. "I did tell you. I told you both. I told you three times and then you forgot."

Bane blinked down at me. "What?"

"You heard me, or have you forgotten what I just said already?"

Ryker stepped forward. "It has to be some kind of magic. Some power we don't understand."

"Come with me," the Sanguinata said.

"Are you out of your freaking mind?" Ryker said. "Why the heck would we go anywhere with you?"

"Fine, then stay out here and die. I, for one, believe the only chance of survival against these creatures is if we work together. Already, we are down three Lupin and three Sanguinata. Our numbers are dwindling, and those gates will not open for another thirty-six hours. Plenty of time for these shadow riders to hunt us down."

We needed to work together and come up with some kind of plan. "I'm in."

"Serenity?" Ryker warned.

"No, she's right," Bane said. "The game no longer matters. What matters is outwitting this new opponent, and I'm afraid it may take all of us working together to do it."

We needed to get going. "We have to warn the rest of the Lupin."

The Sanguinata's throat bobbed nervously, but he nodded. "Agreed."

"And how will we get them to remember what we tell them?" I pointed out. "Unless they see if for themselves, they'll forget."

The Sanguinata tapped his head. "It's up here. I can show them."

What did he mean? "How does that work?"

"Sanguinata can both read and project their memories."

Of course. Dorian had mentioned being able to read another sanguinata's thoughts the first time I'd met him.

Bane headed toward the river. "Their base is this way."

With a glance back the way we'd come, I quickly followed.

The cabin was huge, sturdy, and looked well-maintained.

I nudged Bane. "Why couldn't we have found a base this nice?"

He snorted. "Because it's in a shit location. Look at it. It's exposed for anyone to find." He strode forward.

The Sanguinata hung back, scanning the clearing warily. "I wouldn't be so quick to—"

Bane let out a surprised bellow as he was whisked off his feet and up into the air. He swung suspended from a rope for a second and then curled his body up, grabbed the thick cord wrapped around his ankle, and began sawing at it with his penknife.

My daggers were out in preparation, although I seriously hoped they wouldn't need to taste blood. Bane dropped to the ground, landing in a crouch, just as a neph sauntered out of the cabin. He was too non-hairy to be Lupin but large enough to qualify, because, yep, he was naked.

He stood on the porch, arms crossed. "Well, what have we got here? A Sanguinata and our special guests come for a visit? I knew it. When Dorian petition Jarrod to allow three members of the Protectorate to join the games on some pathetic pretext, I told the boss not to listen. Like any neph would join these games to save a handful of humans. And my suspicions have been confirmed." He speared the Sanguinata with a derisive sneer. "You wanted extra hands. *You* killed our men. You do realize you won't be leaving alive, don't you?"

I held up my hands, free of the daggers now, catching his attention with the movement. "We didn't kill your men. But we know what did, and it's out there, right now. Hunting."

He arched a brow. "There is nothing out there but wilderness and ruin."

"You're wrong," the Sanguinata said. "I saw it with my own eyes. It just killed three of my men."

A shadow of doubt crossed the Lupin's face. "I'm listening."

I filled him in on what we'd seen — on the shadowy riders that couldn't be cut down, and the manner in which they had appeared and vanished so suddenly. And then the Sanguinata stepped forward and closed his eyes. The clearing shimmered and the crazy horseback riders materialized. The memory was vivid and horrific and when it was over the Sanguinata sagged, and clutched his head.

A figure stepped out of the trees to our far left. "Bullshit. Please tell me you aren't buying this shit, Gregory. He could have manipulated that memory."

Great. Another nude, seriously hung neph. At least this one was in hairy mode. Wait, he'd probably been hiding out waiting for the signal to attack us. So, where was the other one? I slid a glance to the right, and, sure enough, a pair of silver eyes peeked back at me from the shadows.

"It's the truth," Bane said. "You know me. You know who I am and what I stand for, and if you listen to your instincts, you'll know we're telling the truth. You don't really believe that we're working with the fangs any more than you think we just walked up to your base with the intention of attacking you."

"Justin, get out here," Gregory called.

The other Lupin stepped into the clearing. "I believe them."

"You would," the hairy to the left said.

"Shut your face, Vince." Justin focused on Gregory. "I told you I sensed something out there. Something dark and new."

Vince snorted in disgust. "You and your fucking sixth sense."

Justin rounded on him. "Yeah, and if you'd

have listened, we wouldn't be three men down."

Gregory held up a hand and the other two stepped back, snapping their jaws closed.

"Say I believe you," their leader said. "What do you propose?"

I looked to Bane, who nodded. "I suggest we work together. We bunk down with the Sanguinata in the manor, we set some traps, and we ride out the next thirty-six hours."

Gregory's eyes narrowed, and then his lips curled in a wicked smile. "I have a better idea. I say we blow the fucking riders to smithereens."

"You have explosives?" Bane asked.

Gregory shrugged. "Let's just say you're lucky you didn't enter the clearing a little to the right."

Fuck. They had land mines. Shit. I cleared my throat. "So, you're in?"

"Yes. We're in."

"If this is some kind of trick ..." Justin trailed off in a growl.

"Shut up, Justin," Gregory said. "Go fetch the explosives."

Justin ducked into the cabin, muttering under his breath, and Gregory climbed down the steps. His body rippled, thickened, and sprouted hair, and damn ... Did his dick get bigger? I tore my gaze away.

The next few hours were going to be interesting.

We made it through the forest without incident and exited onto the open land. It was too exposed here, and we picked up the pace, eager to get back under cover of the canopy of trees ahead. The Lupin loped alongside us, dark shapes streaking across the ground, their powerful bodies sinuous and graceful. They could kill with a single slash of their lethal claws if they wished. Up ahead was the Sanguinata, moving so fast he was almost riding the wind. I could match his stride, of course, but it felt safer to remain in the midst of the pack. We ran solidly for fifteen minutes, but whereas before my body would have protested the exertion, now it reveled in it. A whoop of exhilaration bubbled up in my throat, and I bit it back.

We hit the sparse woodland and followed the Sanguinata as he took us to his base. He led us farther into a thicket and then into an area of hedgerows and brambles until the rays of the moon were blocked out, and we were practically cutting our way through greenery in almost absolute darkness. Finally, we emerged onto overgrown grounds, in the center of which sat a huge, stone building. It had probably been some kind of stately home at one time, and now it was a sad, eyeless monstrosity, waiting to be revived.

The Sanguinata ran around the side of the building and hammered on the service entrance door. Three bangs followed by two short raps and a final bang.

The door opened and another pale face, lit by candlelight, peered out. He balked at the sight of us and tried to slam the door, but the Sanguinata who'd led us here shoved his foot in the frame.

"Wait, don't. They're with me. We need to get inside now." He shoved his teammate back and entered, ushering us to follow.

The interior was musty but dry and surprisingly warm. We were in a candlelit kitchen. A steaming teapot sat on the table and there was even a tray of biscuits. I had to give it to the Sanguinata, they knew how to do things in style. Go to the games, kill a few opponents, and have tea. Wait? Were those china cups?

"What the heck are you playing at, Mal?" the Sanguinata who'd let us in said. He glanced over Mal's shoulder and bared his teeth. "Where are the others?"

"Dead," Mal said. "They're all dead."

"And you led their killers here?"

"We didn't kill them," Bane said. "Neither did the Lupin. There's something else out there."

Another Sanguinata entered the kitchen and immediately went into fight mode—fangs at the ready, body tense and ready to launch.

"Wait." Mal held up his hands. "Hear us out."

The final Sanguinata strode into the kitchen. He was larger than the others with a touch of silver at his temples. He calmly took in the scene and then fixed his gaze on Mal. "You have two minutes to explain why you've brought the enemy into our base, and if I'm not satisfied with your answer, then we will tear out your throat."

Mal nodded. "Of course, Adam. Please read my memories."

Adam pressed his fingers to Mal's temple and closed his eyes. Long seconds passed and then his eyes snapped open. "I've never seen anything like this."

"Same," Gregory said.

Adam locked eyes with the Lupin. "We need to plan how to survive this."

Gregory grinned, the action contorting his Lupin face into something even more twisted and awful. "Forget surviving. We need to kill this fucker."

Adam inclined his head. "Come into the parlor."

The windows were blacked out with thick drapes, the quality of which was at odds with the rest of the shoddy decor. Had they brought drapes with them? Tea and biscuits and drapes? What other creature comforts had they lugged along?

The Lupin resumed their non-hairy forms. They stood with their legs shoulder-width apart, bits dangling all over the place.

Adam sighed through his nose. "Mal, why don't you get our Lupin guests some clothes."

"No, thanks," Gregory said. "Clothes are an encumbrance."

"Maybe so, but we do have a lady present."

Wait, was he talking about me? Yep, he was looking at me. "I'm fine. It doesn't bother me."

Adam shrugged. "Very well." He turned back to Gregory. "You have explosives. So, what do you intend to do with them?"

"Set up a perimeter." Gregory shrugged. "If they try to get in, they get blown up. Simple. We wait out the thirty-five hours we have left, and then we get the fuck out of here when those gates open."

It was a good plan, but the success hinged on them being susceptible to explosives. "And what if the explosives don't stop them? They seem to be able to turn to shadow at will. What if they can avoid the blasts?"

"We worry about that when the time comes," Gregory said.

It was fine as a short-term plan, but we needed a long-term one. "Okay, say we manage to survive even if they can't be harmed by the explosives. What do we do once we're out of here? This thing is obviously new to Arcadia. It probably slipped in through one of the cracks that are forming around the city."

Adam perked up. "So, the rumors are true. The magic that is holding us captive is breaking down."

"I wouldn't say breaking down," Ryker said. "But there are fissures forming. And new creatures from whatever lies outside are slipping through."

Adam licked his lips. "If we can capture these shadow riders, maybe we can force them to show us how they entered. Maybe we can leave."

He looked so hopeful, and bursting his bubble was gonna hurt. "There is no exit. The fissures are one way."

His eyes narrowed. "And you know this how?"

"We have it on good authority," Bane said.

Arachne was good authority? I suppose she was the only authority on the subject. The thought had crossed my mind, and probably everyone else's who had been there that night, that she may have been lying to us. But there had been something open and sincere about the creature that couldn't be denied. She'd openly admitted she wanted to kill us. There had been no subterfuge on her part in that regard. She'd been unapologetic about her nature. No. She'd been telling the truth. And even if she hadn't, what good would it do to go hunting for cracks we may never find? Better to focus on the end game—on winning the experiment between the Black Wings and the White Wings.

The conversation had carried on around me as plans were made to evade the shadow riders, but no one had addressed my original question. "Hey! Hey. How the heck do we stop this thing once we're free of the games? We can't let it go rampaging through Midnight. It's bad enough that we have the scourge to deal with without adding this to the list of our problems."

Bane nodded. "She's right. We may not have a solution now, but we need to work together once we leave here to find one. There must be something in the archives about these shadow riders. A way to stop them. A way to kill them."

"Agreed," Gregory said. "For now, let's go with the explosives plan."

The Lupin set off to plant the mines around the building, and Adam rubbed his hands together. "Seeing as we're going to be here for a while, would anyone like some tea?"

I pulled myself up off the sofa. "I'll pass. I'm gonna make a sweep of the building, if that's okay? Get a lay of the land, just in case the explosives do fail to hold them off."

Adam inclined his head. "Be my guest."

I wandered out of the parlor into the dark hallway. No candles here. And not much heat either. The hallway was cluttered with furniture, and the front door was barred shut with thick planks of wood. Okay, that was one exit out of commission. No problem. It was time to make a memory map.

The Lupin had retreated to the kitchen, the Sanguinata to the parlor, and Ryker, Bane, and I floated in between. The hours ticked by without attack, and the group was growing more and more agitated.

Was this even real? Was it some kind of plot after all? If not for the fact that Mal had seen the shadow riders with his own eyes, we'd probably have been thrown out on our arse. And, to be honest, it looked as if Gregory, the Lupin leader, was gearing up to leave anyway.

"Maybe it won't attack here," Bane said. "Maybe it only runs in the wilderness."

"Which is good for us," Ryker pointed out.

"Yes. But it also means that the Sanguinata and Lupin might conclude that the threat isn't actually real."

Ryker shifted from foot to foot. "The Lupin are getting antsy."

He'd noticed that too.

Gregory strode into the parlor. "We're going for a run. We'll make a sweep."

Adam's jaw tightened. "If you think I'm letting you out of my sight now that you've planted those explosives, then you're sorely mistaken."

Gregory's chest rumbled. "Try and stop us, fang."

Oh, shit. "Whoa. We're all in this together, remember."

"In what?" Gregory snapped. "It's been almost five hours and nothing has happened. We *need* to run. For all we know, these riders have already moved on."

Bane intervened. "Adam, you know the Lupin nature."

Adam licked his lips and strode over to a sideboard where a decanter of dark fluid rested. He poured a glass and downed it.

Blood. He was topping up on blood.

"Fine, go, but—"

An explosion rocked the room. Bane grabbed hold of me, pulling me into his arms to shield me from a threat that wasn't even inside the building.

Ryker smiled wryly. "Bane, the explosion was outside."

Bane cleared his throat and released me.

The Lupin burst into action, heading for the kitchen and the exit to check for carnage and the dead. Another explosion erupted, from around the front of the house this time, and then one more sounded from the east.

Gregory came rushing back. "They're circling the building and setting off all the mines."

I rushed to the nearest window and tugged back the drapes to peer outside. The ground a few meters from the house looked like a bomb had gone off, which it had. But there was only disrupted soil and no visible body parts.

I dropped the drapes back into place. "They aren't affected. We need to run. We need to go now."

Adam looked thrown for a second and then his jaw flexed with determination. "Sanguinata do not run. We stand and fight."

"Sorry, Adam," Mal said. "In this case, I'm all about the running."

But there was no time to get the heck out, because the sound of a horn filled the room and then the shadow riders galloped in straight through the damned wall. More poured in from the kitchen, cutting off our main exit.

A flash of a face, the curve of a jaw, the tip of a sword, and the glint of an eye—they were material one moment and ethereal the next. Ghosts that could solidify at will. The Lupin attacked and the Sanguinata defended, but it was futile because they weren't able to get in any blows. Gregory ducked and defended, Adam leapt and evaded. I had to help. Maybe more bodies attacking would force these riders to slip up. I stepped toward the chaos and Ryker grabbed me around the waist, hoisting me off my feet.

"What the heck?"

"We need to get out of here," he said. "We can't fight this thing."

I jerked in his grasp, and he released me abruptly. He had a point. "I'm not leaving without the others." I scanned my mental map. "The front door is barred, but there is a roof exit we can use." Thank God I'd done a sweep earlier.

A roar of pain had me whipping around. Gregory jumped back to avoid a second bite from a silver whip, but his step was unsteady. I rushed forward and grabbed him just as he sagged. With my arms hooked under his armpits, I dragged him out of range.

"Move, everyone! Upstairs now!" My voice cut sharply through the ruckus, deeper and harsher with my demon giving it an edge.

Gregory stared at me in surprise, and then one of the other Lupin took over from me in supporting his leader. A second later, we were all running up the stairs with the horsemen at our heels. The roof exit was on the third floor, through a bare room with stark floorboards and past a set of French doors. The wall beyond the balcony was hugged by a trellis, as if this room had been designed with sneaky visitors in mind.

I ushered Gregory out onto the balcony with his Lupin supporter. Mal followed with the other Sanguinata. And then the shadow riders exploded into the room. Bane pulled me out of the way just in time, but Adam went down in my place. A rider loomed above him. The flash of hooves pawed the air in a descent of death. My daggers were in my hands before I could think. I slipped from Bane's grasp, slid between Adam and the phantom horse, and brought my daggers up and then down in a V motion, slashing at the shadows. Something warm and wet slapped against my face, and an eerie scream shattered my eardrums.

The horse dematerialized and the riders paused in their attack. Adam got to his feet and slowly reached out to touch my face, his fingers coming away smeared with crimson.

"Serenity, you hurt it," Ryker said. "You fucking hurt it."

It was as if a momentary ceasefire was in effect. All eyes were on me, but then I locked gazes with a rider. His face was wrapped in fabric, leaving only his burning eyes visible, and in those eyes, I read the conflict: flee or fight.

There was no way they were getting away. With a chilling battle cry of my own, I ran at them. Bane's bellow of horror was a vibration at my back, and then my body was swallowed by darkness, and the world was suddenly gray. I swirled into motion, and just like in training, the daggers became an extension of myself. With my eyes closed, my instincts took over and guided my body. The drag of my blades, the snag and the spatters that stung my face, told me I was hitting my mark. My head echoed with screams, and then a melodic male voice cut through it all.

"Cease. You may cease your attack."

My feet faltered.

Strange words I didn't recognize rose up to cover the screams and wails, and then silence reigned.

I opened my eyes, and the riders were gone. In their place stood a tall male with long hair that fell about his shoulders in a tangle of leaves and bracken. His face would have been beautiful, regal even, if it hadn't been covered in grime. His clothes must have been fine once, if the embroidery was anything to go by, but they were worn and tattered now.

Bane appeared to my left and Ryker to my right.

The tension in the air was palpable, shock and anger, and the come-down from an almighty adrenaline rush. It was in the tremor of my hands and the shallowness of my breath.

Gregory was the first to break the silence. He shuffled back into the room, clutching his wounded abdomen. His question was concise and to the point. "Who the fuck are you?"

With the hunt gone, we made our way back downstairs. The stranger came with us, sandwiched between Adam and Bane—not that he was going to be running off anywhere; the guy could barely stand, let alone walk. We sat him on the sofa, and he broke down into pathetic sobs.

"Shit," Ryker said. "What do we do?"

Adam whispered something to Mal, and the fang wandered off into the kitchen.

I crouched to the man's level. "Hey. Can you tell me who you are, and how you got here? Are you connected to those shadow riders?"

He took a shuddering breath and wiped at his eyes with his sleeve. "I'm sorry. Look at me. I'm a mess, crying when I should be offering my thanks. Thank you. Thank you."

He was clutching something, a gem of some sort, his knuckles so white that it was obvious he meant never to let it go.

"Who are you?"

"Oleander. My name is Oleander, and my quest is finally at an end." His body shuddered.

"Quest?"

"To capture the Wild Hunt." He swayed and closed his eyes. "Tired. So tired."

"Mal, where is that tea?" Adam barked.

Mal appeared with a cup of tea and pressed it into Oleander's hand.

The newcomer stared at the cup warily. "Is this a potion to kill me?" He shrugged. "I suppose after all this time running, death would be a relief."

Wow, he really had been through the wringer. "It's just tea. It will make you feel better."

He took a tentative sip, and then his eyes fluttered closed. "Oh. Oh, my. That is good. So very good." He slurped down the rest and licked his dry lips. "You do me two kindnesses this day. First you aid in the capture of The Hunt, and then you break my fast with this wonderful concoction. What is it again?"

"Tea."

"Yes. Tea. A true marvel. It has been centuries since I partook of food or drink."

Wait, had I heard right? "You've been fasting for centuries?"

He nodded slowly. "It has been my curse for setting The Hunt free. The Hunt is a force of destruction, a weapon of war." He held up the jewel. "And a long time ago, I foolishly unleashed it on the mortal world. My people, visitors from another dimension, left me here. They cursed me to follow The Hunt and witness its atrocities until the day I was able to catch it and trap it. I have traveled your mortal world over and over following in its wake. I have heard the myths be born and evolve, and had almost given up hope until we stumbled into this pocket of reality. This hidden place where I finally met you." He held out his hands as if to cup my face, and I jerked back. His hands were seriously filthy. He curled in his fingers. "My apologies. I am overcome. I've always been a step behind, until today. Today you gave The Hunt pause, and that pause allowed me to utter the words to force it back into its prison." He bowed his head. "I am in your debt."

"Where are you from?"

"A place of starlight and rainbows, of bone, ash, and blood. A place that feels like a dream and sometimes can become a nightmare. But it is home."

"You're one of the ancient ones, aren't you?" Bane said. "The race the sea dwellers are descended from."

"Yes, many of our kind who favored the ocean procreated with man. I too considered it, but I was distracted by ... other things. And then I made the most horrific error and have paid for it ever since." He smiled. "But now. Now, I can finally return home."

He thought he could go back to his world and his people. Poor fucker was in for another shock.

Bane and I exchanged glances. He cocked his head in a *should I tell him or will you* gesture.

I pinched the bridge of my nose. "Oleander. I'm afraid there is no way out of Arcadia once you're inside."

He blinked at me for a long beat. "No way out?"

I shook my head. "I'm sorry, no."

He pulled a dagger from the folds of his clothes. Bane shouted out a warning, but I was frozen in place. It didn't matter, though, because there was no aggression in his eyes, only resignation as he plunged the dagger into his chest and yanked it back out, unleashing a spurt of blood.

My body broke from the grip of paralysis. "No. No. What have you done?"

He slid off the sofa onto the floor and into my arms.

"No more. No more." His words were a reedy whisper.

Oh, God. The blood. So much blood. I pressed my hand to the wound. My eyes stung as his sorrow, his fatigue, and his desperate yearning for home swelled inside me. He'd made a mistake, a stupid mistake, and instead of helping him to rectify the error, instead of helping him to hunt this Wild Hunt, his people had abandoned him in a land that was not his own. They'd cursed him. He didn't deserve any of this, and he certainly didn't deserve to die.

His eyes fluttered closed and a long sigh escaped him. He was dying and it was wrong. So wrong. He had to live and make up for all the time spent running, otherwise what was the point?

"Serenity. He's gone," Bane said softly.

"No."

"Serenity."

"Leave me alone." I shrugged off his hand and gathered the wretched creature closer. He was here. Still here. I could sense his essence in the air, hovering. I had to stop him. He had to come back.

My hands grew warm, a different kind of heat, not the sting that heralded the daggers but something new and powerful. It was energy but the kind I'd never felt before. It seeped into my hands, coming from everywhere, from the very air around me, and then my hands began to glow. The light sank into Oleander and his eyes popped open as he took a sharp breath.

He looked up at me in bewilderment. "Oh. Oh, my. What did you do?"

I slowly removed my hands from his chest. His tunic was torn and bloody, but the wound had knit. He was alive and whole. A choked laugh escaped my lips. "You're okay. You're alive."

He stared at me blankly for several seconds. His lip trembled, and he covered his face with his hands and burst into tears once again.

"Mal, we're going to need more tea," Adam said. "And maybe some shortbread too."

My teacup was almost empty, and the kitchen was getting cold, but my body was loath to move.

It was almost time to head to the gates. With The Hunt gone, we all slept like the dead — fang, hairy, and Protectorate all under the same roof; who would have thought, eh? The few hours after healing Oleander had been awkward. Wary, curious glances from the Sanguinata and the Lupin seared the back of my head. I was the woman who'd wounded the shadows and then brought an ancient one back to life. But all I could think about was Drayton. I'd had this ability all along, this ability to manipulate Aether and pull a soul back from wherever it was headed and shove it into its body. I could heal the dead, but I'd been useless to him. The rest, all my other accomplishments today, meant nothing, because when it had mattered the most, I'd failed.

Bane joined me at the kitchen table,

scraping back a seat and lowering his huge frame into it. "You couldn't have known. There is no point dwelling."

How did he always sense what was bothering me? "I know."

"And we still don't know how it works. It could be a one-off."

"I know that too."

"But it's impossible not to wonder, isn't it?"

"Yeah." But there was more. "I sensed his essence when it left his body. I knew he was going, and I pulled him back."

Bane locked gazes with me. "Yes. You told me that."

I caught my bottom lip between my teeth. "I didn't sense Drayton's essence. What if ... What if he wasn't dead when I left him?"

Bane blinked slowly. "Serenity. You were certain he was dead a few days ago. Don't doubt your instincts now in the face of this new revelation. Besides, who knows if this ability has only manifested because you've finally become one with your demon?"

"In which case, I wouldn't have been able to help Drayton anyway."

"Or sense his soul."

Did he really believe that, or was he just trying to make me feel better? It didn't matter, I'd take it. I'd take whatever to stop this awful cramping pain in my mind.

He picked up an empty cup and turned it over in his hands. It looked like a toy between his fingers. "You were brave last night. You saved lives, and you refused to quit. Remember that."

Why was he saying this stuff? Oh shit, of course. I'd failed in the main objective to save the humans from the House of Vitae.

I ran a hand over my face. "I needed a win, Bane. I needed to save the humans. And now Dorian owns me."

"No. I won't let that happen. He'll have to go through me to take you, and trust me, he won't want to do that. You're Protectorate. You're one of us. With regards to the humans, there will be plenty more opportunities to win. Plenty of chances to save human lives."

Adam padded into the room. "It's almost time to go. Are you ready?"

I nodded. "Yeah. Let's get the heck out of here."

We were minutes away from the gates trundling open, and my chest was tight with disappointment. All those humans ...

Adam walked over to me and pressed a bag into my hands. "Take it."

"What is this?" I took a peek and the band around my chest loosened. "Your flags."

Adam smiled. "No. Your flags. You saved

my life. It's the least I can do."

"But don't you need the humans?"

Adam snorted. "I prefer my donors to be willing. Happy humans produce sweeter blood."

"And the others?" I glanced over his shoulder at Mal and the other fang.

"We're in agreement."

"So are we." Gregory handed me two flags. "Here. Take these too."

My throat was all clogged now, and the back of my nose stung. I would not cry. "Thank you." My voice cracked, and I cleared my throat. "This means the world."

"Yeah, well, it's a one-off," Gregory said roughly. But there was a twinkle in his eye.

"It's good to see you in clothes."

He chuckled and leaned in to whisper, "And I'd be happy to see you out of yours."

My neck heated and my cheeks grew hot. Shit.

Ryker stepped between us; the move was casual but clearly a back-off signal. Gregory winked and stepped away.

"You got your flags," Bane said. His gaze was speculative, almost somber.

"That's a good thing, right?"

Bane inclined his head. "I hope so. I really do."

This was about the balance thing. Sanguinata needed blood and humans needed protection. Giving the humans the option of breaking the contract could reduce the Sanguinata's food supply, and hungry fangs could be dangerous. But winning the challenge against the White Wings was more important, and with this victory, we'd given some humans back their free will.

"Well, the Sanguinata will just have to start treating their donors better, won't they? Happy donors will mean less turnover."

Bane blinked in surprise and then let out a bark of laughter. It was the first time I'd heard him laugh, and the vibration of it travelled straight through me and down to my toes. It lit me up from the inside and made me want to lean in to him and trace the laugh lines on either side of his mouth. What the heck was wrong with me? But before I could examine this revelation in any more depth, the fizz of the gates died, and the doors began to slide open.

The last time I'd crossed this moat, I'd been with Drayton. Was he watching over me now from wherever neph souls went? Did he know that I'd succeeded in achieving what I'd set out to do? I should feel triumphant and satisfied, but there was only emptiness, because when all was said and done, he wasn't here to share this moment with me. He wasn't here with his teasing smile or his lazy drawl.

"He would have been proud of you," Ryker said. "I know he was against you doing the games, but it was mainly because he cared about you too much. But if he could see you now, he'd be proud."

He steered the bus we'd hired through the entrance to Dorian's castle and parked up in the courtyard. It was optimistic, I knew. But I was hoping to fill it with humans for the return trip.

"Let's just get this over with." I grabbed

my flags and climbed out. Adam would have delivered the news of their loss to Dorian by now — we'd all agreed to keep the shadow riders a secret. They were gone and there was no point giving Dorian a loophole. The games had been pronounced a draw between Lupin and Sanguinata. Both had come out three men down and with no flags. We'd smuggled Oleander out once the human officials had made their head and flag count and recorded it in their ledgers.

The ancient was now ensconced at the MPD mansion until we figured out what the heck to do with him.

Dorian's butler appeared beneath the arch that led to the entrance to the building. He inclined his head, turned on his heel, and clipped off.

Ryker shot me a look.

"We're supposed to follow."

The journey was familiar, the same corridors and the same staircases. My mental map flipped open in my mind, and the gaps in this route were filled in as we walked. He led us to the same chamber where Drayton and I had seen Dorian before, where we'd witnessed his brutal treatment of his humans.

The doors swung open to admit us, and Dorian sat up straighter on his throne. Even from this distance, his rage was evident in the harsh lines of his face and his stiff posture. Dorian obviously didn't like to lose. My impulse was to slip into goading mode. To plaster a smug smile on my face and take what I'd come for. But my win had only been possible because of Adam and Gregory. They'd given me the flags. They'd liberated these humans, not me.

Speaking of Adam ... He stood to Dorian's right, his head bowed. Dorian tapped his fingers on the armrest to his throne.

"Well, come in. Gloat and do what you must." His tone was light, but his eyes were like flint.

"I'm not here to rub my win in your face, Dorian. We had a deal, and I'm merely here to see that you deliver your part of it."

He studied me through slitted eyes. "You are, are you?"

"Yes. I've heard that you're a man of your word. That you're an honorable neph, and I am here to witness that for myself."

Man, Drayton would be so proud of me right now, with the pretty words and the diplomatic attitude.

Dorian relaxed a fraction. His elbow was resting on the armrest, and he made a backwards wave with his fingers. "Of course, that is simply my nature."

The gathered fangs twittered in agreement.

"Jeffery, bring the humans who have expressed a wish to be released."

The butler hurried off.

"I blame myself," Dorian said. "If I had

chosen a better team, then you would not be standing here claiming victory today. If my team had done their job ..." He slid a sideways glance toward Adam. "Is that not correct, Adam?"

Adam raised his head and a gasp caught in my throat. His face was a swollen, bruised mass. One eye was completely fused shut and the other was bulging and red.

I took a step forward. "What did you do?"

Dorian stared at me sharply. "Why do you care?"

I grit my teeth. The fucker suspected something. No point giving him fuel for his suspicions. "I care because I'm not a sociopath."

Dorian let out a bark of laughter. "There she is. The feisty neph I spied on your first visit. For a moment I thought your lover's death had sapped all your fire."

His words cut through me to the pain buried beneath the bluster. "Drayton was not my lover. He was my friend."

That dismissive wave again. "Whatever. Drayton was always weak. Always trying to play the peacemaker, the diplomat, and look where it got him. It got him killed."

"Serenity, don't bite," Ryker warned.

But blood was the roar of an angry sea in my ears, and Ryker's words were carried away on a tumultuous wave. "Drayton was ten times the man you will ever be. You think that pimped-out chair makes you some kind of king?

No. It's these poor deluded Sanguinata that do that. They either haven't realized what a poison you are, or they're too frightened to admit it. But when they do, when they wake up and realize that they all feel the same, then that pretty throne will be whipped out from under your butt, because the way you're going, soon you won't have any humans signing up to be donors." I turned away from him and addressed the gathered fangs. "The law has changed. Humans can dissolve their contracts, and if you don't start treating your donors better, then you'll starve. Do you understand me?"

Another murmur flitted over the crowd.

"Scaremongering won't work on us," Dorian said. But he didn't sound too convinced.

The doors behind Dorian opened and Jeffery filed in followed by humans. Lots of humans. A gasp went up from the crowd.

Yeah. I rest my fucking case.

The blonde who'd implored me on my last visit spotted me and broke from the huddle of humans to come running down the red carpet toward me. She flung her arms around me and squeezed.

"Thank you. Thank you for coming back for us."

My eyes pricked, and I wrapped my arms around her and hugged her back. "It was my pleasure." I locked gazes with Adam over her shoulder, and his lips, although busted and bleeding, lifted in a painful smile.

The humans came toward Ryker and me.

"It's a good job we brought a bus," Ryker said.

I smiled.

"Take them. Go," Dorian snapped, and then to the humans, "House Vitae protection is no longer upon you. You'll die out there. You and your families."

The blonde girl rounded on him. "No. We won't die. We have the Protectorate."

"Oh, boy," Ryker muttered.

Our entourage spilled onto the bus, and then we were off, over the moat and up the drive toward the gate. The humans huddled in silence until we slid off Vitae grounds, and then a collective cheer went up.

"Thank you," the blonde girl said.

I glanced back at her. "What's your name?"

"Ava. My name's Ava." Her eyes gleamed in triumph. "And we won't forget what you did for us." Her emerald eyes glittered with gratitude and something more...the beginnings of a plan?

The bus bumped over a pothole and Ava fell back into her seat. I fixed my eyes on the road.

Ryker grinned. "You know, this actually feels really good."

Warmth infused me. "Yeah, it really does."

It was almost time for Drayton's memorial service. Taking a deep breath, I headed out of my room and down the corridor toward the main staircase. A door to my left opened and Cassie strode out.

She stopped at the sight of me, her mouth parting in surprise.

Thank God she'd come back for the memorial. A smile tugged at my lips, and I took a step forward to give her a hug, but then my gaze fell to her hands, which clutched a small overnight bag bulging with clothes.

"You didn't come for the memorial, did you?"

She snapped her mouth closed and stood tall. "I thought everyone was already out back."

"You were waiting for us to leave so you could sneak in and back out again?"

She rolled her eyes. "You make it sound so clandestine."

"Isn't it?"

"Whatever." She turned away. "I'll be back for patrol tomorrow, but I can't stay here."

"You're seriously going to ditch on Drayton's memorial?"

"I don't need a memorial to remember Dray."

"Cassie?"

I glanced back to see Orin standing at the

other end of the corridor, his face pale and drawn.

Cassie faltered, and for a moment, I thought she'd turn back, but then she pushed her shoulders back and continued to walk away.

Orin made a strangled sound, part pain, part rage. Fucking hell, how many times was she going to break his heart? But when I turned to him, his face was composed and stoic.

"Let's get out there. It's about to start," he said evenly.

I nodded and followed.

We gathered under the stars, our dark clothes blending into the night, heads bowed in deference to our fallen officer. This was the Protectorate's farewell to one that had been with them for a long time. It was a farewell to Drayton.

We couldn't hold a funeral without a body, so this memorial would have to do. We hadn't needed to go far, just out back into the grounds, where an obsidian pillar etched in golden script had been erected in memory of Drayton.

Bane walked up to the pillar and turned toward us. His face was shadowed with sorrow. "Drayton was an honorable neph. A moral man. He was our friend, our brother, our family, and he will not be forgotten. His death shall not be in vain, and The Breed will pay for what they have done."

A murmur of agreement rose up from the crowd.

Ryker laced his fingers through mine, and Orin slid an arm around my waist. Rivers stood on the other side of Ryker, his gaze fixed straight ahead.

"Drayton, you will forever be in our hearts," Bane concluded.

There was a long moment of silence and then slowly the gathered began to disperse, and then it was just Ryker, Rivers, Orin, Bane, and me.

"We'll get them," Orin said softly. "We'll make Max pay for what he did."

Ryker squeezed my hand.

Bane walked toward us. "We will. But not tonight. Tonight we say goodbye to our fallen comrade. There's a bottle of single malt in need of emptying, and a lasagna in need of preparation."

Yes. Tonight was goodbye, and there was someone else who should be here saying goodbye. Except she couldn't be. I'd need to go to her.

I looked up at Orin. "Hey, fancy driving me somewhere? There's something I need to do."

The cemetery arch stared back at me from

beneath a starry sky. It was clear up here, fresh and peaceful.

"Would you like me to come with you?" Orin asked.

I shook my head. "No. I think I need to do this alone."

He crossed his arms and leaned back against the car. "No problem. Shout if you need me."

I walked up the rest of the incline and under the arch into the cemetery proper. A hush fell over me like a comforting blanket, and the ache in my heart seemed to ebb just a tiny bit. The mausoleum stood open in front of me, surrounded by pretty fireflies, and distant music played, drifting out like tendrils of smoke to meet my ears.

"Viola? Viola, are you there?"

The fireflies hovered toward me and then veered away into the mausoleum. What had Viola said the last time? Something about the fireflies telling her that Drayton was here? Were they delivering a message to her now? Telling her I was looking for her. Okay, maybe I was just being fanciful. Should I go into the mausoleum?

I took a step toward it.

"I wouldn't do that if I were you," a male voice said.

I spun to find a young man leaning up against an elaborate gravestone. His clothes were strange, old-fashioned, and his hair was combed to the side in a style that hadn't been used for decades.

"Why not?"

"It's invite only. I could invite you, if you like?"

"And why would you do that?"

He shrugged. "Curiosity. Why do you want to see Viola?"

"That's between me and Viola."

"Is it about Drayton?"

"Who are you?"

"Name's Lennie."

"And you're dead."

He laughed. "Well, yes. Can't you tell?" He went all see-through.

Funny. "I just need to speak to Viola."

"You do?" Viola said from the mouth of the mausoleum.

I turned to her. "Hi. Thanks for coming."

Her gaze slipped over my shoulder. "You came alone?" She blinked in confusion.

"Yes. I have … I have some news." Oh, shit. How to say this.

Her eyes widened. "It's Drayton. Something has happened … He's hurt."

I licked my lips. "Viola, Drayton is dead."

Her hand flew to her mouth and she stared at me in horror. "No. You're lying. He sent you here to lie to me. To force me to move on and forget. How could he? How could you?"

My eyes grew hot and my nose began to

run. "I wish I was lying. I wish it hadn't happened, but it did. He died, and I killed him."

She shook her head in horror. "No."

So I laid it on the line: the kidnapping, The Breed, the cage, the beating. I told her it all. She fell to her knees and Lennie picked her up, cradling her against him as she sobbed as if her heart would break.

"That must have been hard for you," Lennie said. "You didn't have to come and tell her."

I swallowed the lump in my throat. "She deserved to know. He'd have wanted her to know that he loved her."

It may not have been entirely true, but if it gave her comfort then what was the harm. She turned her face into Lennie's shirt and sobbed harder.

"I'm sorry." I turned to go.

"Wait," Viola called out, her voice thick.

I glanced back.

"It wasn't your fault. Drayton wouldn't have wanted to hurt you. You did what you had to."

I'd heard these same words so many times since Drayton's death, but for some reason, coming from her, they were like a soothing balm on my fractured soul. This time, when I walked away, she didn't call me back.

Orin greeted me by holding open the passenger side door. "Done?"

"Yeah. I'm done." I climbed in and tucked my hands into my pockets. It was cold, even with the heater on. Something hard brushed my fingers. I pulled it out of my pocket, stared at the white business card in my hand. So much had happened. My power was evolving, and with Ambrosius being silent, it was impossible to tell what aspects of my power were related to my demon and what were related to the daggers. Marika had promised answers. The Order knew what the daggers really were. The question was: Could I truly trust her?

Orin started the engine. "Bane's cooking tonight." He shot me a cheeky grin. "If we get home on time, we may catch him in his apron."

I gripped the dashboard. "Then what the hell are we waiting for. Step on it."

To be continued …

Join Serenity as she continues her adventures in *Secrets of Midnight*.

Scroll down to check out the first chapter.

The district council had provided cheap plastic chairs that scraped over the floor as attendees seated themselves. Langley, the head of the MED, stood by the entrance that would admit the chief council members, his lips turned down in disapproval. Several other MED officers dotted the room—a precaution, just in case proceedings got volatile.

"This is your fault," Bane grumbled.

Urgh, this again. I rolled my eyes. "I do not control the minds of humans. Not one of my skill sets."

He made a harrumph sound. "You should have shut her down immediately. As soon as she came to you with the preposterous idea."

"It's not preposterous to want to take your fate in your own hands, to want to protect yourself."

He made a sound of exasperation in the back of his throat. "They're humans. Fragile, mortal beings, easily crushed, chewed up, and spat out."

"All the more reason to give them the power to fight back. Come on. You must see the benefits for Midnight if humans could fight back against the scourge and The Breed."

He sighed, his powerful chest rising and falling, stretching the fabric of his shirt so taut I was afraid it would tear under the strain at any moment.

"Seriously? Do you get your clothes custom-made?"

He shot me an are-you-fucking-kidding-me look.

I shrugged. "It's a reasonable question."

The humans had settled down, waiting eagerly for the proceedings to commence. Bane and I leaned up against the wall opposite Langley, halfway down the room. The door beside Langley swung open, and five humans came striding in. They climbed up onto the podium at the front of the chamber and settled down behind a long desk. It all looked very official, but it was a farce, because how the heck were they gonna stop the kind of movement that one woman was starting—a movement that I was totally behind, by the way, and if I was honest, I was developing a serious crush on the instigator of this event.

The doors at the back of the room slammed open, and the woman in question entered. Ava strode in, tall, blonde, and defiant, her head held high. This was the woman who'd fought back against Dorian, who'd broken his compulsion and moved me to help liberate the contracted humans from House Vitae's grasp. It had been almost six weeks since that day, but we'd been in contact ever since, and she'd come to me over a week ago with this idea, this venture that was a passion shining in her emerald eyes. Man, how she'd changed from the scrawny thing Dorian had been feeding from. She'd put the weight back on, turned it into muscle, and was looking pretty kick ass in the threads I'd helped her pick out for the event. The boots were kick-the-shit-outta-you hot, and the leather jacket was just sexy. Eight other humans walked behind her, dressed in black, hair slicked and coiffed, and looking dangerous. Yeah, they certainly looked the part they were asking permission to play—a human Protectorate. Fuck the MED who sat behind desks and pushed paper. Fuck waiting for the MPD to show up to save the day. No. These humans wanted to take action, and damn,

I needed pom-poms and a cheerleader outfit real bad right about now.

I recognized several faces, all humans that had been held hostage by Dorian and his Sanguinata. They knew what it was like to feel truly powerless, and they were here to demand authority to do something about it. They wanted to form a unit, to train with the MPD, and work alongside us in keeping Midnight safe. Bane, being Bane, was less than impressed. He saw it as having to babysit humans while trying to save all the other humans. The man was most definitely a glass-half-empty guy.

But empowering the humans was surely the way forward? And if we were all about the free will, then surely we needed to support the humans in this.

Ava walked past us, dropping me a wink on her way to the front of the room.

Bane snorted in disgust. "Yep, this is your fault."

Okay, so maybe I'd encouraged her a smidge. But where was the harm in that? In my humble opinion, there should be no need for jumping through hoops. If humans wanted to band together and form a unit to fight back against the terrors of Midnight, then fair play to them. I was all about the empowerment, and Bane could carry on looking like he'd sucked on Lilith's sour tits for all I cared.

"The council won't approve it," he said

smugly.

"God, you sound like that wanker, Langley. They can't stop us from moving forward with this."

"Us?"

"I'm helping no matter what the outcome."

"Of course you are, Harker," he said dryly. "Because insubordination means nothing to you, does it? Why don't you teach them that, eh? And then watch them get killed, because a unit is only as good as its chain of command."

Ouch. He had a point. Time to swallow my pride. "I'd like to help them regardless, if that's all right with you, boss."

"We'll see."

Was that a smile tugging at the corner of his mouth?

The room fell into silence, and the central council member, a somber-looking, middle-aged woman, began to speak.

"Ava Love, you have petitioned the council for the authority to form a defense unit made up of humans. Is this correct?"

"Yes, ma'am," Ava said.

The councilwoman scanned a piece of paper on the desk before her. "Permission to use lethal force against hostile nephilim, including, but not limited to, the scourge and The Breed."

"Yes."

"And you state that you have the support of the MPD in this endeavor?" She glanced across at Bane, who remained impassive.

I nudged him sharply in the ribs, and with an exasperated sigh, he nodded.

The councilwoman turned her attention back to Ava. "Miss Love, you are asking the council to permit you to put your life and the lives of your fellow humans at risk."

"It's better than being powerless and getting picked off every month," Ava replied tersely.

The councilwoman's lips tightened. "It is also extremely dangerous, like agreeing to send a group of lambs into wolf territory. So, tell me why should we grant such a petition?"

Ava crossed her arms under her breasts. "With all due respect to the council, this is merely a formality that the MPD insisted I go through. Whether you give your permission or not, we, as the citizens of Midnight, have the right to protect ourselves."

Oh, man. This was specifically what I'd advised her against. Ava Love had a tendency to get mouthy, and her recent stint as Dorian's blood bag had lit a fire of vengeance and determination inside her that could easily flare out of control. It was one of the reasons why, when she'd come to me asking for help on this project, I'd agreed. She was a laser without a focus, a weapon without a target. Yeah, she needed this, but challenging the authority of the council was a dumb move, and the downturn of the councilwoman's mouth told me she was about to deliver a smackdown.

It was time to step in, but a member of the public beat me to it.

"And what if your actions rile up The Breed and the scourge?" a young, heavily pregnant woman said. Her face flushed, whether with embarrassment from all the eyes on her or in indignation, I wasn't sure. "What if the change prompts them to increase their attacks on Midnight? Why try to fix what's working? The MPD and the MED have been keeping us safe for years. The Houses provide ample protection during scourge runs and from The Breed."

Ava's shoulders tensed.

Bane snorted. It was his *I told you so* snort. The man didn't have to speak to communicate his annoyance, derision, or disappointment. He had snorts to do that for him, and the fact that I could decipher them was kind of worrying.

The councilwoman waved the pregnant lady down, but a man at the back stood up. "She's right. This is the last thing we need. We have things under control. The casualties are minimal. Why rock the boat?"

The councilwoman raised her brows and sat back. "Well, Miss Love, would you care to respond?"

Ava pressed her lips together, her eyes flashing dangerously. She turned to face the crowd. "Why rock the boat?" Her tone was incredulous. "This isn't a boat, this is our home, and we need to stand up and protect it. The MPD can only do so much. They can't be everywhere at once. Have any of you stopped to wonder how hard it must be for them to cover the whole district every month when the scourge attacks?" She focused on the guy. "Minimal casualties doesn't cut it. There should be zero casualties, and with our help, the MPD may be able to achieve that. I'm done being a victim, and it's about time you stopped thinking like one too."

A low murmur skittered over the crowd and several heads began to nod in agreement. The councilwoman's lips twitched.

Bane sighed. "Damn it."

"Ava Love, the council grants you authority to form a unit, but active duty will only commence once the MPD has signed off on your training."

Langley's face was a picture of incredulousness.

The councilwoman scrawled something on the paper and then held it out to Ava. "There you go, Miss Love. I look forward to hearing about your progress. It's about time we made some changes in Midnight. Less paperwork and more action." She slid a glance Langley's way, and his eyes narrowed.

Ha. Looked like I'd misjudged the councilwoman and the council, but for once, I was glad about being wrong.

The council representatives filed out and Langley followed, probably eager to try and change their minds. It wasn't that he disagreed with the unit. It was more the fact that its existence made the MED look bad. Like, why hadn't they come up with this idea? Or why was it necessary in the first place?

Ava strolled toward us, her face alight with excitement. "Did you hear that?"

Bane pushed off the wall and brushed past her. Damn, he was so not happy. He'd probably been banking on the council shutting this down. Great. I'd have to soothe the bear. Shame he didn't like honey.

"You did great, Ava."

She winced. "I almost blew it, didn't I?"

"Yeah, but you pulled it back."

"So, when can we start training?"

"Come by tomorrow. We'll make a start. The scourge runs again in three weeks. I think we can have you ready by then."

"Why not today?"

I glanced over her shoulder at the door that Bane had just pushed through. "I have a few things to sort out first."

She followed my gaze. "Boss still not completely on board, eh?"

I winced. "Sorry."

She pushed back her shoulders. "Well, we'll just have to show him that we mean business."

Yeah, and I needed to make sure he was going to be there to see it.

Other books by Debbie Cassidy

The Gatekeeper Chronicles
Coauthored with Jasmine Walt
Marked by Sin
Hunted by Sin
Claimed by Sin

The Witch Blood Chronicles
(*Spin-off to the Gatekeeper Chronicles*)
Binding Magick
Defying Magick
Embracing Magick
Unleashing Magick

The Fearless Destiny Series
Beyond Everlight
Into Evernight
Under Twilight

Novellas
Blood Blade
Grotesque

The Shadowlands Series
Coauthored with Richard Amos
Shadow Reaper
Shadow Eater
Shadow Destiny

About the Author

Debbie Cassidy lives in England, Bedfordshire, with her three kids and very supportive husband. Coffee and chocolate biscuits are her writing fuels of choice, and she is still working on getting that perfect tower of solitude built in her back garden. Obsessed with building new worlds and reading about them, she spends her spare time daydreaming and conversing with the characters in her head – in a totally non psychotic way of course. She writes High Fantasy, Urban Fantasy and Science Fiction.

Connect with Debbie via her website at debbiecassidyauthor.com and also catch her on twitter -twitter@authordcassidy.

Made in the USA
Monee, IL
11 December 2023